D1045174

THE
MARVELOUS
MISADVENTURES
OF
INGRID
WINTER

Center Point
Large Print

**This Large Print Book carries the
Seal of Approval of N.A.V.H.**

THE
MARVELOUS
MISADVENTURES
OF
INGRID
WINTER

J. S. DRANGSHOLT

Translated by TARA F. CHACE

CENTER POINT LARGE PRINT
THORNDIKE, MAINE

This Center Point Large Print edition
is published in the year 2018 by arrangement with
Amazon Publishing, www.apub.com.

Previously published as *Ingrid Winters makeløse mismot*
by Tiden Norsk Forlag in 2015. Translated from
Norwegian by Tara F. Chace. Originally published in the
United States by Amazon Publishing, 2017.

ISBN: 978-1-68324-753-1

Library of Congress Cataloging-in-Publication Data

The Library of Congress has cataloged record
under LCCN: 2017061395

To my family

Where are you heading? Everything is already here.

Ted Hughes

1

The marimba ringtone was not to be ignored. I tried mental calisthenics for a couple of minutes to see if I could block out the noise with brainpower, but I fairly quickly conceded. I opened my eyes and tried to figure out what day it was. It felt like Wednesday, a little too far into the week and still too far to go until the weekend.

I rolled onto my side.

"Are you going to shower first?"

"No," I said.

"Why not?"

"I'm going for a run."

"You are?"

Pause.

"No."

I hung my nightgown on the already over-crowded hook on the back of the door, climbed into the tub, and just managed to back away from the spray of cold water. The original floor plans had included a shower enclosure across from the tub, but we had nixed that.

"We want to put the shower in the tub," I had explained to the plumber at the planning meeting, "to save space."

"Are you sure?" he'd asked me.

"Yup."

"Well, you should at least put in the underlay for the shower stall," the plumber had objected, "in case you ever sell the place and the future buyers want a shower. It's smart to think down the road a little bit."

I remember I'd considered calling Bjørnar to see what he thought, but he had already made it quite clear that he was too busy to attend these meetings. So I had carte blanche to do as I pleased.

And I knew what I wanted. Our future was in this house. This was the end of the line. We were building a home right where we wanted to live, one with the perfect number of bedrooms and living rooms and a small yard where we could grow rhubarb and plant roses and a cherry tree.

So I'd smiled at the plumber a little condescendingly and reiterated in a decisive voice that we wanted the shower *in* the tub. With no underlay for a future shower stall. Period.

Then a year after we moved in, Alva was born. Suddenly the house felt crowded and loud, as if we were all up in each other's business all the time. This feeling was reinforced when Jenny had to give up her room and move in with Ebba when Alva turned one. There had been arguments every night since then. Should the window be open or closed? Did they want the light on or off? Were they going to read or not? Who was the quietest sleeper?

"Ebba breathes too loud when she sleeps," Jenny complained. "It's gross!"

"Well, Jenny farts! Yuck!"

Plus it was impossible to get the rhubarb to grow big and luscious. No matter how much I fertilized it, there were only a few tough, skinny stalks that no one ever ate. And I couldn't get the roses to bloom. We never even got around to buying the cherry tree.

And exactly two weeks after we moved in, Bjørnar brought up that business about the shower stall.

"A shower stall," he said. "We should have put one of those in. Why didn't we think of that?"

I stood there staring at him, but didn't say anything.

"A shower stall," I finally repeated.

"Yeah, that would have made sense. Did you know the neighbors have one? They said it was included in the original floor plans. Did we veto it or something?"

"No."

"It wasn't in the plans?"

"No."

"You're sure?"

"Yes."

"Hmm, well, it should have been. I don't like showering in the tub."

"Why not?"

"I just don't like it, standing in the tub. It's

9

not . . . pleasurable. Plus you have more arm room in a shower stall."

"Really? But what about all the room we have now? I mean, now we could fit a cabinet or some shelves in here. We wouldn't be able to add those if we had a shower stall."

"We should've put in a shower stall."

As this grew in scale from a mere disagreement into a full-blown argument, the way these things do, I started to doubt that this house really was the end of the line for us. Maybe it wasn't the home we were going to grow old in.

In the beginning I only checked "Houses for Sale" once a week, but soon the online real estate listings became the first thing I clicked on in the mornings and the last thing I looked at at night.

Not that it made any difference. It was always the same houses in the same neighborhoods at the same prices.

We agreed that the lack of selection wasn't a problem and that we had plenty of time, but secretly I was starting to worry it was already too late, that we'd passed too many restaurants and now we were going to end up at McDonald's.

The warm water ran down my body. Some of it formed puddles around the outside of the tub. I closed my eyes and tried to empty my head as I walked my fingers over my breasts to check for lumps. As usual it was impossible to tell what was normal mammary tissue and what wasn't.

Bjørnar came into the bathroom.

"You should mop up that water!" he said. "I don't know what we were thinking. Why didn't we put in a shower stall?"

"I don't know," I mumbled. "It really should have been included in the floor plans."

"Anyway, we're late," he said. "Are you going to wake up the kids?"

"Could you feel this one breast? I wonder if there's a lump in here. Kind of over here, right by the armpit."

"No way! Now go get the kids up."

I shook the two eldest awake and carried a half-asleep Alva, who still smelled like a babyish mixture of milk and rubber, downstairs.

Inexplicably, Bjørnar had already had time to set the table, put out an assortment of fruit, and place slices of bread on each of the plates.

"TV," Alva mumbled, her pacifier still in her mouth.

"No TV now, honey. We're eating breakfast."

"I'm not honey."

"I know that, sweetie. But you have to eat up now, because we're going to preschool soon."

"Is it Monday?"

"No, it's Wednesday."

"Thursday," Bjørnar corrected me.

"Thursday. And tomorrow is Friday, and then it'll be the weekend."

11

"When's tomorrow?" Alva asked.

"After today."

"Tomorrow is after today?"

"Yes."

"Huh. Can I use the iPad?"

"OK."

She zoned out, focusing intently on the screen while raising spoonfuls of Cheerios to her mouth with one hand and holding the other under her chin to catch any dribbles. Jenny stared blearily out the window. Ebba was putting cherry tomatoes into her lunch box one by one. Bjørnar was reading the paper across the table from me and wrinkling his nose at the fair-trade coffee. It did taste like muddy water.

I drank them in with my eyes.

This was it.

Right now, when everyone was relatively content and no one was screaming because they had to put on their jacket or shoes. Right now, when everyone was present and no one had remembered they had PE or swimming yet. This moment of harmony and peace. Of security. I wanted this to go on and on, to last.

But then I started thinking that someone actually did have PE or swimming today. And then I noticed Bjørnar glance at the time and I knew the moment was already over.

The way it's always already over.

2

It turned out there was at least a glass of Barolo left in the wine bottle that I had added to the bag to return for the deposit, and when I hoisted the bag into the car, the deep-red liquid drenched my jacket sleeve.

"What's that wet stuff?" Alva asked as I fastened her seat belt.

"Mama spilled some wine."

"Yuck," she said, wrinkling her nose.

I opened both car windows all the way to air out the alcohol smell, which quickly permeated the car.

"Close the windows! I can't hear my show," cried Alva. "Close the windows!"

I didn't close the windows until we were on our way up the last hill, approaching the preschool.

"I didn't get to hear about the spider," she whined as we walked inside.

"You can play it again when we drive home," I replied and set her boots in her cubby before we walked into the classroom.

"Good morning," I said to the teacher in the cheerful voice I always reserved for those whose goodwill I depended on.

"Good morning," she said. "What did *you* bring to school today, Alva?"

"Was she supposed to bring something?"

"Oh, no, she didn't need to. But she *could* have brought something, because it's show-and-tell today."

Alva shuddered and a rock sank in the pit of my stomach.

"I'm sure it'll be fine," I said in a way I hoped sounded casual, running my hand over Alva's cheek. "We'll just bring something the next time."

"But I wanted to bring Fluttershy!"

"I know."

For a few seconds I considered going home and getting the plastic horse she was referring to, but I put it out of my mind.

"We'll just bring an extra toy the next time you have show-and-tell," I told her.

She stared up at me with her big, wet eyes. I smiled encouragingly, set her on the teacher's lap, and practically ran out into the hallway, where Alva's classmate Rachel was busy pulling things out of her bag and putting them into her cubby.

"Look what I have," she told me, and proudly pulled out the red horse with the green mane whose twin lay abandoned and alone in the toy box in Alva's bedroom.

"Fluttershy," I said.

"What did Alva bring?"

"Nothing."

"Why not?"

"I don't know."

"Do you want to see what I can do?"

"No."

"Why not?"

"I don't know."

"What's that smell?"

"I don't know."

"I smell something . . . Yuck, what is that?"

"Wine," I said tiredly.

"Wine?"

I was about to explain about the bottle and the deposit and the Barolo when the teacher stepped into the hallway.

"Are you still here?" she said to me.

"Apparently so."

"Alva's fine. Karen brought two ponies, so Alva can borrow one of hers."

"That's great news! Next time I'll have to put show-and-tell day on the calendar," I said with a laugh.

She smiled back, but it didn't seem entirely genuine. That made me nervous.

"Time for breakfast," she said, diverting the owner of Fluttershy, who ran up to her, whining.

"Bye," I said. As I walked out the door, I just barely overheard Rachel saying, "Alva's mommy smells like wine."

Traffic on the highway was backed up and only creeping along. When I finally reached the office, I immediately stuck a note on my door that said "Testing in Progress" and started writing the conference paper I was already late submitting. I heard people approach my door several times throughout the morning. I listened to their shuffling footsteps and could sense their desperation as they stood outside my door. Desperate for someone to talk to, someone to complain to about lazy students, the bureaucratic nature of the administration, dishonest colleagues, rejected manuscripts, or inhumane workloads.

Sure, Monday was usually the worst. Over the weekend, a backlog of agitation and anxiety would build up, and faculty members might need long-term paid sick leave to recuperate if it didn't get vented. And yet Thursdays were bad, too, because they were so close to Saturday that they got people's eyelids and the corners of their mouths twitching. Which is why there was an unwritten rule in the department that Thursday was the day for encouragement and collegial camaraderie.

Usually I made time for it, because being a part of this workplace demanded small talk and commiseration. But not today. Today I broke the rules and sat silent as a mouse, holding my breath, waiting for the desperate people to shuffle along. Maybe that was wrong of me, but I just wasn't up to their doom and gloom today.

The ones in high heels moved on right away,

but the most pitiable ones—the ones in sneakers, loafers, or sandals with socks—stood there for a while. I could hear their breathing through the door as they lingered, listening to make sure there really was testing in progress, until they eventually sighed heavily and moved on toward the break room or the copy room.

Despite these measures, I only finished about half of what I had planned to get done, and when I left I had to stuff my organic cotton bag full of folders and books so I could do some more work later at home.

It wasn't until I walked past the open door to the meeting room and noticed Peter Walsh in there carrying teacups that I recalled the reminder that had been blinking in my calendar for a good week.

"Ah, we seem to be the first ones here," he said to me.

"Huh?"

"Everyone else is late. *Late!* I don't know why we don't just set all the meetings to start at a quarter past. We're brainwashed into thinking only in academic quarter-hour blocks of time. Why don't we just accept that?"

"Oh, right . . . ," I said. "The meeting. Actually I have to, uh . . ."

"There you are!" said a voice. "In you go." The chair of the department gave me a gentle nudge from behind so I stumbled into the windowless

17

meeting room, where one by one the rest of the department quickly materialized. I knew I had to speak up now, right away, and say something. I could not be a party to this. I opened my mouth, but then closed it again.

I hated meetings. I hated the pointless discussions, the trite, predictable sense of humor, the endless digressions that dragged on ad nauseam, and the crazy compulsion to bring up and discuss every last little thing and squeeze it in under "other matters of business."

That's why we hardly had a single meeting when I was the faculty coordinator for the department. I received almost daily e-mails back then questioning why we never had any meetings, along with suggestions about topics we could meet about, but I just hit "Delete" and pretended I hadn't ever seen them. They should have been as happy as clams to get out of all those meetings. They should have thanked me for making the tough decisions on my own and letting them spend their workdays working: writing, publishing, providing guidance, and teaching, all the stuff we were actually being paid to do.

The result was that I was stripped of the title.

"I think it would be best if we let someone else take over as faculty coordinator for a while," the chair had said contemplatively. "There have been complaints, you see, reports that people's sense of community in the department is taking a hit. People miss having a forum for dialogue."

That's because people use these meetings as an excuse for not working, I thought. And I wouldn't have it.

I hadn't attended a single meeting in the department since being asked to step down as coordinator. Until now.

I stared lugubriously across the table, where Ingvill was taking her seat. Her hair was gathered into two scrawny braids that hung limply from either side of her head. They dangled when she leaned forward, like little mouse tails. She set down her phthalate-free thermal travel mug, which she had bought at a conference in Germany and which could almost be considered a bodily appendage.

During my stint as faculty coordinator, she had implied several times that I ran things with authoritarian tendencies. The chair had mentioned that as well.

"I'm not saying that you do," she had said, "but if people perceive it that way, we have a problem."

"Ingvill thinks everyone has authoritarian tendencies," I'd said. "That's what her life is based on. She's a perpetual victim."

"Who said we were talking about Ingvill?" the chair had responded.

I watched Ingvill now, slurping coffee out of

her eco-friendly mug, pulling out a gray pencil eraser and a sorry notepad she had procured from the supply closet.

"I see that we're all here," said the chair. "So, to get right down to business: As some of you already know, we've been instructed to revise all our course offerings. Whether we are for or against this, the fact is that the College of Arts and Letters passed a resolution and now we need to follow up. Thus, there's no point in discussing the merits of the revision. The only matter of business at this juncture is a practical consideration of how to organize our programs and which classes to cut. And this needs to be done quickly, preferably by the end of the semester."

A sigh ran through the room, creating a vacuum that made my scalp tingle. I only had five minutes and they were running out.

Ingvill had managed to take a half page of notes in her notepad already. She was probably psychoanalyzing herself. In Ingvill's universe there was only one person. The rest of us were props.

Peter raised his hand.

"May I remind you," he said, "that the last course revision was only two years ago."

"Yes, in a sense that's correct," the chair said.

"So . . ."

"So now we're implementing a new one."

Peter sniffed disapprovingly.

"What do we need to do?" Ingvill asked nervously.

"First of all, we need to increase the number of credits for our courses so that we're better aligned with the rest of the Norwegian university system."

"May I remind everyone," Peter said again, "that two years ago we reduced the credit weighting for all the courses for that very reason?"

His voice quivered in indignation, and the chair began to quickly enumerate all the excellent reasons for the credit realignment. She came off sounding impartial, but it was no secret that she, along with many other members of the administration, would have preferred to have a university without any faculty members at all. They found us annoying, argumentative, overly neurotic, and generally useless. The dregs of the university system.

As I watched Ingvill, it occurred to me that you couldn't really blame them. As the chair's list grew steadily more complicated and elaborate, her face grew increasingly pinker and her thoughtful expression deepened. Eventually she looked completely flummoxed.

"But as I said, this meeting is just for informational purposes," the chair concluded. "Now you know what needs to be done college-wide.

The administration is asking that we take this back with us to the department and figure out where to make cuts and how to accomplish the restructuring."

I turned on my cell phone to check the time. I could still make it. If only no one said anything now.

I held my breath.

"What will this mean for internationalization efforts?" Frank asked.

I saw Peter put his hand over his eyes and I wanted to thunk my head on the table. The chair smiled triumphantly. Everyone knows that *internationalization* is to the university what *ecumenical* is to the church. Whoever brought up this concept automatically got points for taking the conversation seriously, no matter what we were talking about, but whoever answered the question would *also* win brownie points for their familiarity with institutional priorities.

The chair responded with a long and unnecessarily detailed response about how many foreign students this reform might bring in, and Frank nodded attentively and took notes on the notepad he had brought. I glared at him. He was wearing some kind of a shark-tooth pendant on a leather cord that hung over the front of his sweater.

Who did he think he was fooling? I studied his scrawny arm, holding his pen, and thought how easily I could take him in a fight. Take ahold of that little head of his and bring my knee up into his face until his nose and forehead were bleeding.

He looked up and our eyes met. I looked away.

"If it's good for internationalization, I'm all for it," he told the chair. "After all, we have a duty to live up to the Bologna Process by helping to harmonize higher education throughout Europe. As you may know, I was recently selected to serve on the committee that will travel to Saint Petersburg to work specifically toward achieving some sort of bilateral cooperation."

The chair seconded this with a nod while I rolled my eyes, even though I'd been specifically banned from doing just that.

"We don't roll our eyes, no matter how dumb we think other people are," the chair had informed me during our little chat. "And perhaps we might all benefit from giving a little thought to the possibility that we might not always be entirely infallible?"

"What are you trying to say?" I had asked.

"Excessive contact with students?"

"You heard that from Ingvill, too," I hissed.

"No comment."

"A student brushed my arm! And it was meant tongue in cheek!"

"That's what *you* say. We have had instances of sexual harassment involving students here in the past, before my time. I have two years left now in my tenure as chair and I will not, I repeat *not,* have any of that under my watch. Is that clear?"

"Check," I had muttered. "No sexual harassment."

"You just rolled your eyes again!"

"Fine. No sexual harassment or eye rolling, even though the very idea of something like that is completely absurd. Have you seen what I look like these days? I haven't shaved my armpits since last summer, and it's not because I never wear anything sleeveless. I don't have breasts anymore. I never wear foundation or mascara. I own only one lipstick, which I bought in 1997. I cut my own hair after a glass of wine. And I'm almost forty!"

She had studied me for a moment and then sighed.

"Just quit rolling your eyes so much, OK?"

Occasionally I was able to pull off an eye roll in my mind, but not always, not this time.

The room had grown quiet, and I peeked at the time again. Ingvill was reading through her eight pages of notes. Her mouse-tail braids dangled over the table.

"Couldn't we just revert the courses back to the way they were before?" I asked in an attempt to wrap up the meeting. "Then the problem would be solved. The way they were before the last revision, I mean. We must still have all that information in the system somewhere or other, right?"

Peter made a hiccuping sound that could have been a laugh. The chair looked at him.

"Unfortunately we can't do that, because we no longer have the resources that we used to," she informed us.

"What does that mean?"

"For those who get to stay in the department, it means more work for the same or less pay," Peter translated grimly, "and the rest would be reassigned elsewhere in the university."

"Not necessarily," the chair objected, which resulted in more hiccuping along with vigorous head shaking from Peter. "But as I said, we will need to cut a number of courses. At least three at the BA level and four at the MA level."

"But . . . reassignment?" Ingvill asked breathlessly.

"We're not talking about that now, but it's widely known that they need more people in the preschool-teacher education program."

A shock wave hit the room.

After that a debate broke out, which grew so heated that Peter and two other faculty members stormed out in anger. For her part, Ingvill leaned even farther over her notebook, jotting things down so violently it looked like her braids were having an epileptic seizure.

"I realize this isn't easy, but if anyone has

creative ideas for how we can accomplish this—in purely practical terms—that would be most welcome," the chair encouraged.

I held up my hand.

"Yes?" she said with a hopeful expression.

"I have to go."

"Now?"

"I have a . . . meeting at my daughter's preschool."

"You are aware that even in academia, we do have business hours, right? And that this meeting is rather important for the evolution of our department moving forward?"

"Yes, sorry, but I have to go."

I stood up with an apologetic smile, searching for any hint of approval or acceptance, but had to leave before there was any. That was what happened when you hung up a sign that said "Testing in Progress" on a Thursday.

3

It had been pouring since early that morning, and even at this hour the highway was a Middle Earth serpent of slow-moving vehicles. I drummed my fingers on the steering wheel and cursed the spineless bicyclists for deciding to drive the second a little precipitation started dripping from the sky. A song about fields of gold was playing as I pulled up in front of the preschool and turned off the radio.

"Mommy!" cried Alva when I finally entered the room where they kept the children whose parents weren't on time for the annual pancake fiesta. Alva threw the half-dressed, one-armed Barbie doll she had been holding aside and asked, "Do we get to eat, too?"

"We're going to buy some pancakes," I told her.

"But are we going to have food?"

"Yes, pancakes."

"And food?"

"And food."

I took hold of her soft miniature hand and we walked into the common room, where three large tables had been set up in front of one of the windows. The tables were covered in trolls the kids had made by hand. Alva picked one with yellow and black hair, pink button eyes, and a white nose, and I handed her a ten-kroner coin to slip into the empty plastic ice cream container meant for the payments.

Listening to the clank of that coin filled me with such an intense feeling that I had mastered this whole parenting thing that I let Alva stuff herself full of pancakes and juice. I even let her go back for seconds. And thirds. To think of all those years I had forgotten to bring change to the annual troll and pancake sale, so that Ebba and Jenny had had to spend hours sitting in the forgotten children's room without a single pancake. But today I had ten ten-kroner coins in my pocket. Third-time parent for the win!

"Are the pancakes the food?" Alva asked, her face plastered in strawberry jam.

"Yes, the pancakes are the food."

"Haven't you ever had pancakes before?" her teacher asked. She was making the rounds selling raffle tickets. She got our second to last ten-kroner coin.

Alva shook her head.

"We make other things," I said quickly. "Cakes and bread and stuff like that, just not pancakes very often. We don't have a griddle at home."

The teacher blinked at Alva and said, "Well, it's a good thing you got a chance to taste pancakes here at preschool then."

I laughed sheepishly and watched the teacher

hold out the raffle basket to other families. Many had turned out in force, with mothers, fathers, and grandparents. The very idea of trying to coordinate a large family showing like that caused a rushing sound in my head.

"Alva, honey, we have to get going," I mumbled, running my hand over her back.

"Why?"

"We have to pick up Jenny and Ebba from their after-school club. Oh, and then we can show them your troll."

Alva nodded. She carefully picked up the last pancake from her paper plate and ate it in small bites on our way out, to savor the culinary marvel as long as possible.

The cloakroom was empty except for Titus and his new Filipino au pair, whom his parents had recently hired so they could trade "quantity time for quality time."

"Up until now," Titus's father had explained, "I've been a servant in my own home. I do the preschool drop-off, I make dinner, I work out, I clean the house. That's not the kind of life I want. I want to spend quality time with my children, not stress out about stuff. So we're getting an au pair."

"That's super," I'd said. "Really. Neato."

Now Titus was standing there chanting, "Pancakes, pancakes, pancakes, pancakes," while the au pair slowly and patiently tried to put on his jacket, hat, and shoes.

My first instinct was to try to vacate the cloak-room as quickly as possible, but then I decided to be a mensch and contribute to the lives of others. It was Thursday after all.

"There's a party today," I explained to her, in Norwegian.

The au pair looked up, confused.

"What?" she said in English.

"There's a party today. They're collecting money for an orphanage in Colombia. The kids made trolls for us to buy. They cost ten kroner each. Do you know what trolls are?"

I made a troll face and said, *"Waa ha ha!"* but that just made the au pair jump and take a couple of steps back.

"Sorry," I said, "I didn't mean to scare you. But there's also food. They have a little café today. They're selling a kind of Norwegian pancake, too. They're called *lapper*."

"Oh, OK . . ."

The au pair continued dressing Titus, who was now chanting "café" instead of "pancakes" and tugging at the au pair's thin hoodie.

"Yes," I agreed. "Café. You should go, for his sake. Anything else would be selfish."

She slowly turned around and stood there looking at me, in a way that felt almost accu-satory. But I was just explaining how things worked, helping her be a good au pair. She should be thanking me, instead of giving me a look.

I made a point of sighing loudly, then picked Alva up and exited the cloakroom.

"I don't like Titus," Alva said as we walked outside. "He's mean."

"Maybe there's a reason he's mean," I said.

4

By the time we parked at home, Alva was asleep and Ebba and Jenny were arguing. I had no idea what about. These spats usually started as statements and accusations but quickly descended into a kind of barking. Variations of sounds that grated on the bone structures in my cranium, continually weakening it and rendering it less impervious to diseases and madness.

The instant I released the child safety lock, they each immediately opened their doors and darted out because they both wanted to be the one to get the mail. I stayed in my seat and listened to Alva's heavy breathing, staring at the wall of the carport until I eventually took a deep breath and turned to face the violins, sheet music, lunch boxes, wet swimsuits, gym bags, and the sleeping three-year-old.

I picked Alva up and pulled the pacifier out of her mouth. It was probably time for her to give it up, but I wasn't up to starting that project.

"We're home now, honey. You have to wake up."

No reaction. Her head rested heavily against my shoulder and her breathing was deep and regular. Once we were inside I put her down on the floor and gently shook her.

"We're home now, honey. You have to wake up."

She opened her eyes a crack, but they immediately slid shut again. Her head lolled forward and her legs buckled under her. I shook her harder.

"Alva, you have to wake up. Otherwise you won't be able to fall asleep at bedtime tonight. Alva!"

With a howl she twisted out of my arms and took a few wobbly steps. I followed her and tried to give her a hug, but then she kicked and howled even louder.

"Honey," I said and kissed her on the cheek.

She whined quietly, "I want crackers and milk! And Diego!"

"Sure."

I carried her to the sofa, smelling her soft hair and feeling a tug at my heart, as if a thin thread were being pulled through it.

"Lovely, lovely Alva," I murmured and laid her down.

"Crackers."

"Yup. Do you want a blanket?"

Alva nodded, and I covered her with a blanket and turned on the TV. I should have tried to get her started on something more active, get her to play with her sisters, get out the art supplies or beads. Or maybe something more gender neutral, like blocks. Instead I turned up the volume on the TV and headed for the kitchen.

A vague sense of frustration quivered in my chest.

I should go for a jog. That would put my humors back into balance. Reduce the level of black bile. It had been a while now, over a week.

But I didn't have it in me. My body felt weak, soft like jelly.

Which is why I chose instead to unload it all on Bjørnar as he stood over the cutting board later, his sleeves rolled up and with that wrinkle in his forehead that didn't usually go away until late in the evening.

"I got so irritated," I concluded, "both at the au pair, who clearly doesn't care, and at Titus's parents, who just renounced all responsibility for the whole preschool. *Quantity time?* What does that even mean? That's what it's like for *everyone*. That's life! I know that it's mostly their fault, but she could have shown a little interest, couldn't she? I was just trying to help! I was being a mensch! And it's her job to take care of the kid!"

"Don't you think maybe she had other things to think about?" he asked calmly, walking over to the sink to rinse the brussels sprouts. He usually parboiled them, then sautéed them in sunflower oil and sprinkled them with sea salt. My mouth was watering at the thought.

"What do you mean?"

"Well, where did you say she was from again?"

It wasn't because I didn't follow the news. I

34

considered myself a relatively well-informed person and I had seen countless TV images of cities, pulverized and destroyed by the inconceivable and gruesome forces of nature.

So it wasn't that. I just hadn't made the connection. The distance between the preschool and the natural disaster was so vast. They were like two satellites orbiting their own end of the galaxy.

Until now.

I thumped my fist against my head and pursed my lips.

"Doesn't it embarrass you to be so self-absorbed?" Bjørnar asked.

"It didn't occur to me that she was from the Philippines," I mumbled.

"It might make sense to think a little before you speak."

"But I live locally," I protested. "If you start looking at life from a global perspective, I don't know how you can bear it: natural disasters, war, poverty, human trafficking, pornography, and prostitution. The Western world's exploitation of development-challenged countries. I can't think about all that on a daily basis. I don't have the bandwidth!"

"*Development-challenged?* Is that even a term?"

"Well, I think *third world* is kind of outdated, if that's what you're thinking."

35

"You get that you're going to have to apologize, right?"

"To the au pair?"

"Yeah."

"Do I have to?"

"Yes."

I stared out the window. At our cherry-tree-less yard.

"Fine," I sighed. "I'll apologize."

I probably had to.

Yeah, I had to.

But only if I ran into her. Because if I didn't run into her, it would be physically impossible for me to apologize. Even Bjørnar had to concede that.

5

The next day I left work directly from the reading center to avoid the meeting room. Just in case. Earlier in the day I had run into Peter, who was all up in arms.

"Do you know the University of Bergen just lowered the number of credits their courses are worth?" he announced and then made a hiccuping sound, which seemed to have become chronic. "Which is the opposite of what we're doing. What we're doing is just a way to cut back on staffing. Mark my words!"

"What do you mean? Are they going to lay people off?"

"Lay people off, reorganize, offer incentives . . . Who knows what form it will take? This administration isn't really calling its own shots, if you know what I mean. They're going to get a taste of their own medicine, though."

"Uh, what do you mean?"

"Oh, you'll see," he said, nodding knowingly, "you'll see."

That exchange created small ripples of uncertainty in my mind. After all, I was one of the most recent hires. If anyone was going to be re-orged, there was a good chance it would be me, especially after my lackluster performance as faculty coordinator. Plus, I hadn't published all that much since I'd started here, either.

"Zero point seven points," the chair had told me. "That might do during the honeymoon period, but it won't cut it over the long haul. We're evaluated based on our output, as you know. The bibliometric indicator system may not be the soundest system in the world, but fair or not, it's how we are assessed right now."

I had nodded vigorously, but the fact of it was that after completing my dissertation I wasn't really up to starting a new research project. My plan was to put off the problem by signing up for conferences now and then. Then at least I would have *something* to pull out of my hat. Though the conference I'd received a grant to attend was still a few months off, it was already starting to bug me. The plane could crash. I could be raped and murdered. I could get stress cancer from excessive dread beforehand. To put it succinctly, my life could be torn asunder. All in the attempt to score a few idiotic career advancement points with my department chair and a colleague who hardly knew what my name was and certainly had no idea what my research interests were.

Luckily it wasn't raining and the bicyclists were back doing their thing again, so there was less traffic. In just under half an hour I was able to carry a beaming Alva off the playground and into the hallway, where I immediately started stripping off her hat, mittens, rain gear, fleece jacket, and wool socks.

"You came to get me before snack!"

"Yes, sometimes I pick you up before snack."

"But not always."

"No, not always."

"Not on Saturday."

"No, but there's no school on Saturdays. Now we have to get your bag."

Only then, when I looked up into the cloak-room, did I notice Titus's au pair digging around in his cubby.

And I'd gotten here early. To be on the safe side.

I straightened up and took a few steps forward.

"Hello," I said, smiling uncertainly.

The au pair jumped.

I took another step in her direction and held out my hand. Not to touch her. More to show her that I meant well.

"Ahem . . . about yesterday. It didn't occur to me that you were from the Philippines, but of course you are. And they just had a typhoon there, I know that. Is everything all right with your family?"

Up until the last sentence it didn't seem like she understood any of what I was saying, but at the word *family* the muscles in her face started contracting. Her eyes filled with tears and her lips began to quiver.

"I have no contact," she said, her voice trembling. "One week. I cannot reach."

Wind started blowing inside my head.

Tears began pouring down her cheeks, and I suddenly felt the need to offer her some helpful advice. Hadn't they said something about Twitter on the radio? Something about the names of people who were accounted for being tweeted?

"Do you have a Twitter account?"

"Who?"

She had pulled out a tissue and was now trying to mop away the enormous tears still running down her cheeks.

"Twitter. Social media."

"Twitt?"

"Twitt-er."

"Twitt?"

"T-W-I-T-T-E-R. The Internet. There are lists or something like that there. Ask your family."

"I cannot reach."

"I mean your host family, Titus's parents. They can help you. With Twitter."

Shut up! a voice in my head was screaming. *Stop going on and on about Twitter!* But I couldn't stop, because I didn't know what to do. Should I hug her? How do people in the Philippines feel about personal space? Is hugging OK?

So, I just repeated the bit about Twitter while she tried to calm down.

"Do a search on Twitter," I said, "not Twitt."

"I try to call!"

"No, you can't call Twitter. It's on the Internet."

"I pray," she said.

"Yes." I nodded. "Prayer is good. Very good."

We stood there for a moment without saying anything, until Titus started tugging her arm and I agreed with relief that it was time to go.

6

All the attention I had paid to the pancake party and the au pair had resulted in my being even further behind on my conference paper, so on Monday morning I was up at five. I stacked the books from my office in a big pile next to my laptop and planned to open them as soon as I checked Facebook. I always did this, even though the news feed was only ever filled with birthdays and nuggets of wisdom like, "All the days that came and went—I never realized those were life," and pictures of people's kids and Starbucks cups. I sent one birthday greeting and clicked "Like" on three random posts, then moved on to the real estate site, where there were now 289 listings. As expected it was mostly a disappointing mix of "condo in co-op building with large balcony" and "new high-end, modern single-family home."

Everything looked the same. Everything was the same. All the time.

Which is surely why I didn't react right away.

Because it didn't look like anything from real life. So I sat there looking at a picture of a big red imposing house with ivy and crushed white rock in the yard, without really seeing it. "Birdsong in the city," I read, without really taking it in. "Rare opportunity."

And it was only after I had scrolled through two more pages of "new construction, beautifully appointed with nice yard" and then came across the house again that I realized it was actually for sale. Here. In the real world.

My brain started tingling as I read the description and then clicked on the photos of everything we were looking for: family room, storage, bedrooms for everyone, a big yard, an office, a dining room, and an attic. This house even had things we didn't know we were looking for, like an English fireplace, a chandelier, and wallpaper with birds on it. I clicked through the photos again and again, until a bleary-eyed Bjørnar appeared in the kitchen.

"Look," I said, waving him over with a gesture that felt mildly hysterical, "come here! It looks like it came right out of an Astrid Lindgren book!"

And the instant I said those words out loud, I realized they were true. Not Villa Villekulla from *Pippi Longstocking*. More like the house in *Lotta on Troublemaker Street*. True, it wasn't yellow the way Lindgren described it in the books, but it was every bit as crooked and charming and with just as many nooks and crannies and chimneys and a white picket fence and plants in the yard, and yet cleaned up, with nice tile work, modern bathrooms, and wallpaper. And I realized that deep down inside, even after looking at all those minimalist, modernist places, *this* is what I had always wanted. Because no one describes a family Christmas like Astrid Lindgren. No one could capture the beautiful, intimate moments between siblings, spouses, parents, and children the way she did. No one grasped what it truly meant to create a home the way she did.

Bjørnar and I read through the description together.

"A showpiece designed by architect Edvard Brochmann, renowned for his dignified homes for those with discerning tastes."

"A house with a soul," I said with a sigh. Then, "Birdsong in the city." (Again.)

I turned to Bjørnar without breathing.

He looked back at me.

"You do understand that that's not us, right?" he said.

"Not us?" I repeated, confused.

His statement reverberated in my head, until I finally understood what he meant. He meant that a 1919 house was too complicated, too wild, and too much for us to handle. The two of us, who had not mastered practical home repair skills beyond taping and painting. The two of us, who liked to aim horizontally, toward normalcy, routine, and predictability.

The two of us, who had invested everything in not shooting too high or too low.

I knew what he meant.

But this time he was wrong.

"But look at it, would you," I objected. "Look how nice it is! And a ton of work has already been done on it! Maybe it *is* us, and we just don't know it yet? We're always discovering new facets of ourselves. I mean, for example, I never used to like *gjetost* cheese, but now I love it!"

He looked at me without saying anything, and I regretted the analogy.

"It's too risky."

"But it's not *that* expensive. If we got it for the asking price, we'd have a little bit of a buffer, wouldn't we?"

"Maybe."

"I mean, we are looking for a house, right? We need something bigger. We do agree on that?"

"Yeah."

"And there's never anything available! It's right where we want to live. Well, almost. And look how great it is! And practical. It has a shower stall and everything!"

He clicked through all the photos one more time. Blue-and-white-patterned Italian tile in the hallway. Wooden ceiling beams painted in light colors. Big bedrooms with wallpaper. There was a ringing in my ears. He was wrong. Despite all the risks and uncertainty this might entail, it *was* us. We'd just never realized it. We hadn't known ourselves.

The real us. That's what this house was pointing to.

"This is a proper home," I mumbled. "A real one."

He didn't respond.

"Surely we can swing by and take a look at it," I pleaded, "just, you know, go for a walk? Tonight?"

"We'll see. I have to go now. I have an early meeting. You'll handle the kids?"

"Of course."

"I'll just grab some coffee for the road."

"Whoops."

"You didn't make any coffee?"

"Sorry."

He buttered a slice of crisp bread, and I used brainpower to make the water boil in record time, waiting for exactly thirty seconds before pushing down the plunger in the French press. Then I filled an insulated travel mug, including maybe a few grounds, and followed him out into the hall.

"I just thought of something," I said.

"What?"

"If a doppelgänger comes and takes my place, we probably ought to have a sign."

"What kind of sign?"

"Here's the sign: I'll say, 'To be or not to be,' and then you'll answer—"

" 'That is the question'?"

"Correct."

"OK, but that's not a sign. Everyone knows that verse. Anyone else would respond the same way."

"Incorrect. Most people would just say, 'Huh?' "

He looked me in the eye and said, "You know we're not going to buy that house."

I smiled and handed him the travel mug.

He sighed and shook his head.

"We can talk about it later. I'll crunch the numbers a little tonight."

"Great!"

I followed him with my eyes, out into the snowflakes, which had started fluttering down even though it was only October.

"To be or not to be!" I yelled.

He didn't hear me. Or at any rate there was no response.

I should have realized that even that was a sign.

But I guess I wasn't really paying attention.

7

There had been an accident on the highway, and it took me forty-five minutes to get to work. Once I was there I stuck the "Testing in Progress" sign on my door and closed it again. It was risky to repeat this trick. If people saw the note too often, they usually started to ignore it, assuming that I'd probably just forgotten to take it down. Then you run the risk of people completely ignoring it for weeks to come.

But it had been a few days since I last put it up, so I chanced it. I had to finish my conference paper. The organizers had already sent out several reminders. They also wrote, "Based on the information already provided, your paper on 'Tehom' will be part of the Postmodern Feminist Theology panel." Several words in that sentence concerned me. *Postmodern*, for example. Even though the word had been in circulation for several decades, no one really knew what it meant, and conversations about it generally ended up in belligerent bickering. Plus nine times out of ten, academics who used that word in their own writing were obfuscators, filled with hot air.

The other word that made me nervous was *theology*. Although there were several areas in literary-studies circles that utilized theological concepts, theologians were blissfully unaware of this, to the extent that they became indignant every time we used a word they believed they had a monopoly on. The term *amateur* had been lobbed at me several times as a result of just this type of cross-disciplinary terminological misunderstanding.

And then there was the whole feminist thing. Nothing in this whole world frightened me as much as feminists. Even though I *was* a feminist. And not just in theory, either. For example, I'd been buying my girls clothes from the boys' department for ages in order to avoid the overly tight jeans with all the glitter and bows. Plus, I was concerned about semantics and was always careful to use gender-neutral terms like *letter carrier* and *firefighter*. And I tried not to immediately picture a man when I heard a title like *professor* or *doctor*. Plus, I rarely shaved my armpits or legs. And besides, I had devoted large tracts of my dissertation to examining the inherently gendered nature of epistemology and deconstructing and reconceptualizing the materiality of sexual difference.

So I was definitely a feminist.

But it was like that wasn't enough.

Maybe I just wasn't angry enough.

Or political enough.

Or concrete enough.

Anyway, I got the impression they didn't like

me. They usually regarded me coolly and then misunderstood everything I said:

> What do you mean 'post-Tehomic'?
> Why did you refer to Butler, when Braidotti would have been a more natural choice?
> Can you elaborate on why you refer to water as being associated with femininity? That seems to be a relatively essentialist statement.
> Associate Professor Winter, are you perhaps an amateur? *(Again.)*

To be completely honest, all this was nothing compared to the main thrust of my paper, the subject I had spent countless years writing my dissertation on: Tehom.

"The Great Deep," which can also mean "abyss, sea" or "to agitate, destroy, confuse." It comes up right at the beginning of the Bible, as early as verse two. When the earth is a wasteland and a void, and darkness lies over the deep, over Tehom.

Because the Spirit of God may have moved over the formless earth, a void. But there was something that wasn't empty. Something that was already there.

Something that either comes *ex nihilo* or that is *ex nihilo* per se.

Which rests there as itself, in complete darkness.

Which has always rested there, and which is resting there still.

Which slumbers.

Waiting.

Waiting for chaos or nothingness to take over again.

There is no time in Tehom.

No order.

No sense of good or evil.

There is only Tehom.

And it is the scariest thing in the whole world.

I had no idea why I wrote my dissertation about it. Maybe it was an attempt to gain control. Maybe it was an attempt to tackle my worst fear head-on.

The result, though, was that I never got away from Tehom, away from my awareness that it was there waiting for me, the presence of an absence. Or, an absent presence.

The first time there was a knock on the door, I ignored it. But the knocker, who clearly couldn't read, didn't give up.

"Yes?" I said, irritated, to a pimply face.

"Sorry I'm late," the face said, "but I didn't quite understand where it was."

I peered at the unfamiliar face and was trying to send him back out into the hallway when I realized who he was. A persistent high school student who was writing a term paper on *The Hobbit* and who had told me over the phone that he needed "*considerable* help."

"You can stop by at ten thirty," I had heard myself say, "but I have a phone conference at eleven, so I'm afraid you'll have to leave then."

And now, here we were, trapped in a conversation I understood less and less the longer it went on.

"As you know, Tolkien has written a lot of other famous books," he informed me, "but I want to focus on *The Hobbit* since it's so short. Well, that and I like dragons."

"OK," I said.

"So, I was wondering if you could help me."

"With what?"

"With my assignment."

"But help you with *what?* Finding secondary literature? Understanding the symbolism?"

"What's secondary literature?"

I sighed.

"Someone said you had written something about *The Hobbit*," he said.

"Have you read my article?"

"No."

"Have you read *The Hobbit*?"

"No. I thought it was a little slow. But I did watch the movie."

At 11:05, Bjørnar called.

"Oh!" I said, relieved. "That's my phone conference."

He showed no sign of getting up, so I held my hand over the receiver and gestured with my head that he had to get going.

"Good luck with your assignment," I said.

"I'll definitely stop by again," he said. "So you can help me jot down a few things. I'll call you."

"Hi," I said tiredly to Bjørnar.

"This is your own fault," he said. "You have to man up and say no to this kind of thing."

I sighed.

"Couldn't we just fake another phone conference?"

"No, I'm done conducting fake business meetings with you. There's nothing in it for me."

I sighed again.

"Anyway, I'm glad you remembered to call, because I'd forgotten he was coming. Are you going to be home early enough for Jenny's friendship group tonight?"

"I'm going to try. But I have to write that trivia contest for them first. You're handling the prizes, right?"

"Yup," I said.

The friendship group. We were *this* close to not having to do it. When the room parent brought it up at the PTA meeting, I could tell that several people were preparing to say no. But then after Dina's dad, that annoying broker, started arguing

53

against the friendship group and Emma's mother brought up online bullying, everyone was suddenly in favor of it.

And now here we were hosting the thing, and already two kids had been dropped off. Twenty minutes early. They ran into the living room without even saying hello, and started chasing each other around the table. They kept that up until everyone had arrived, when I was able to shepherd them all together and seat them at the dining table, along with rolling pins, flour, cookie cutters, and dough.

"Isn't it a little early in the year to make gingerbread?" asked Matilda, who wore a ponytail high on her head and always adopted a Disneyesque pose in photos.

"No."

"Did you make this dough yourself?"

"Yes."

"When did you do that?"

"Yesterday afternoon."

"What time is afternoon?"

"Later in the day."

"How late then?"

"Five o'clock."

"Do you work?"

"Yes."

"What do you do?"

"I'm an associate professor of literature."

"What's that?"

"That means I work with books. I read books and try to think clever thoughts, and then I write things down, about the books. Read, think, write. That's what I do."

"That sounds boring."

"Yeah, I guess."

Pause.

"Oh, and I also teach. At the university."

"What do you teach?"

"About books."

"*Just* books?"

"Yes."

"No math?"

"No."

"Well, your job doesn't sound that fun. I'd totally rather work in a pet store."

"OK. Do you want me to roll out your dough for you?"

It was sticky, way too sticky. I had to add a lot more flour, and I struggled to remember why I hadn't bought ready-made dough from Ikea. I supposed it was just on principle. Although sometimes I suspected I might have a bit of a masochistic streak.

The other kids quickly tired of waiting for me to finish rolling out the dough, and they started making mountains of flour and rolling dough-clump boulders down the sides, or playing catch with the dough across the table.

"You might not want to split the dough up into such little pieces," I warned, continuing to roll out my own little slab, "if you want to have big enough sections to cut shapes out of."

"Are you a dwarf?" Kai asked me out of the blue.

"No," I said.

"You look like one. My mom is a lot taller than you."

"Should I put on a movie?" I asked.

"We're not supposed to have any screen time during friendship group," Matilda protested. "We're supposed to play with each other and be social."

"Oh, I'm sure it's fine, just one short movie until Jenny's dad gets home. Then we're going to have a trivia contest!"

"Are there going to be teams?" Kai asked, excited.

"No. It's going to be every kid for himself."

"Oh."

"But everyone gets a prize," I hurriedly added, "and the prize for the winner is awesome!"

"Yippee!"

Immediately they started guessing what the first place prize might be.

"Maybe an iPad!"

"*Ooh,* or a gift card to the indoor fun park?"

"Or candy!"

The rumble in my head gained strength. *Did we*

56

have anything that could serve as a prize? I was wondering when a gray car pulled in, and I ran to the door to meet Bjørnar.

"This is painful," I whispered as he stepped inside, "terrible, awful. I hate this! I hate them. You have to help me!"

Bjørnar smiled the way he always did when he came home. As if he were happy. As if nothing could ruin this, the moment when he was finally reunited with his family. It had occurred to me that I ruined this moment almost daily. Because I couldn't wait to unload about how idiotic my colleagues were or about all the things that had gone wrong during the day or about how impossible Alva had been because she fell asleep in the car and had been a pill ever since or about how insufferable it was to listen to Ebba and Jenny arguing all afternoon.

I tried to police this inclination, but very rarely succeeded.

He knew that.

And still, he came home with a smile.

"Hi!" he exclaimed as Alva ran in and flung her arms around him. "There's my Alva! You're so pretty! And so heaaaaavy! Did you guys make gingerbread cookies?"

She nodded seriously.

"Did you make one for me, too?"

She shook her head.

57

"What, no cookie? Oh, then there's going to be some tickling!"

She squealed so loud that it distracted the friendship group from their movie and the kids came to check what was going on.

"Can you do that to me, too?" Jenny asked.

"And me!" said Kai.

"No, you guys are too big. Were you watching TV? I thought there was no screen time during friendship group."

He gave me a look.

"Oh, it was just for a few minutes," I explained. "Should we eat minipizzas and have our contest now? You did make the contest, right?"

"Oh, I made the contest all right," Bjørnar replied seriously, "but it's in written format and the questions are really hard. You guys aren't going to get any of them right."

Even Kai got that this was a joke, and with astonishing speed everyone gathered around the kitchen table.

The rest of the time I served minipizzas and tried to stay out of sight so that Bjørnar would handle the contest on his own. I was both envious of and grateful for the good mood he had put everyone in.

It was as if he didn't find people scary at all. And no one wondered if he was a dwarf.

"Who won?" I asked when the contest was over.

"Jenny actually did."

Jenny raised her hands over her head in triumph, but immediately received a punch on the arm from Kai, who had only managed to finagle his way to second place.

"Ow," she complained.

"Oh . . . but Jenny can't win the grand prize, because it's something we already have. Maybe we could give it to Kai since he came in second?"

"*Yes!* Give it here!"

I handed him one of Jenny's books. She crossed her arms in front of her chest and gave me the evil eye.

"A book?" Kai whined. "I don't want that!"

"What's my prize?" Alva wondered.

"I don't have anything for you, honey," I explained gently. "You're not actually in the friendship group, you know. These are Jenny's classmates."

"You didn't buy anything for the other kids, either?"

Bjørnar looked at me with his eyebrows raised before taking Alva into his arms and giving Kai clear instructions to stop hitting Markus on the thigh.

"You should bike over to the grocery store and buy prizes," he instructed. "And a consolation prize for Alva."

"I don't want a consternation prize," she sobbed. "I want a *real* prize."

"Yes, yes," he corrected himself, "a real prize."

"But what am I going to buy at the grocery store? They don't have anything. Should I get them candy? That's not going to go over well with the parents, is it?"

"I guess you'll find out!"

A few exhausting hours later I was sitting on the edge of Alva's bed, looking at Alva, who was lying on her side, breathing heavily, her mouth open and a little bit of vomit still on her cheek. The friendship-group kids had left with their candy prizes, which had resulted in a text message from Matilda's mother letting me know that on principle she was opposed to the practice of handing out candy at events that weren't birthday parties and that took place on school days.

I wiped Alva's cheek, tucked her in nicely under her covers, and tiptoed out.

"Can we take a little walk over to that house and then have a glass of wine?" I asked Bjørnar, who was at the sink washing cookie cutters.

"No to the first and yes to the second."

"Come on! It's just a quick walk."

"I'm not up to it."

"Oh, please. I've been thinking about it all day."

"*You* can go for a walk."

"I don't want to do it alone. Come on. Just a

quick walk to take a look and decide if we want to see the inside. They're having an open house on Saturday, you know."

He sighed.

"Fine."

We went upstairs to tell the kids.

"We're going to go for a quick walk. Could you guys get in bed and just read? We'll be back soon. Daddy has his cell phone."

"Can we put on an audiobook?" Jenny asked.

"I don't want to listen to an audiobook," Ebba protested.

"Put on the audiobook, but not too loud. You have to be able to hear Alva if she wakes up."

Jenny nodded seriously, and I stared into her unreadable blue eyes and again felt the thread slowly being pulled through my heart.

We bundled up in our scarves and heavy jackets and walked in silence. I loved the feel of the evening air on my skin. It washed away all the grime the day had stirred up. Made everything smooth and clear again.

I took Bjørnar's hand and we moved so effortlessly and harmoniously through the world that I almost forgot the purpose of the walk, until he suddenly stopped and pointed.

He was pointing at a house, one that shone so radiantly that it almost took my breath away.

And I knew I'd been right all along.

This was our home.

There couldn't be any doubt. There sat the house we were going to live in. Not just this year and next year, but when we were so old we couldn't read the paper without a magnifying glass and had to put our dentures in water before we turned off our reading lights.

"Ours," I said.

"It's going to go for way more than the asking price," Bjørnar said, "and we can't afford it. But it is a nice house."

"Ours," I repeated.

"Not ours," he corrected me, "but it is nice."

We stood there in silence for a little while before continuing down the hill.

I saw a woman in the kitchen of the house doing the dishes. A warm light shone behind her. Yet again I had the thought that it was a model home. Something that didn't exist in this world. Something that was too good to be true.

It was dangerous to want things like that, things that actually don't belong anywhere other than fiction. Besides, a little voice inside me said it wasn't wise to rock the boat, reach for too much, fly too close to the sun. But, as so many times before, I didn't really listen.

8

In the days leading up to the weekend, my suspicion was confirmed: the house we were living in now wasn't a proper home.

We had been lying to ourselves this whole time.

And once a fantasy is revealed as fantasy, there's no going back.

Once you've escaped from the chains down in the cave and crawled out into the sunlight, going back in is simply not an option.

The shadows in the cave are just shadows.

Truth and light are in the other direction.

All you have to do is go for it.

There was a knock on the door.

"Yes?"

Ingvill poked her head in, and I rolled my eyes—on the inside.

"Do you have five minutes?" she asked in that plodding way of hers.

"Actually, no," I mumbled, "but you can have twenty seconds?"

She smiled hesitantly and sat down on the chair I kept for visitors.

"It's about this course revision," she began. "I don't think we should accept them."

"We don't really have much choice, do we?"

"I think we do. We've set up a committee to oppose it."

"To oppose what?"

"The course revision."

"What kind of opposition are we talking about?"

"I can't tell you today. Our first meeting isn't until Monday."

"Who's going to meet?"

"The committee."

"Uh-huh. OK."

"That means anything I tell you now is mere speculation."

"I see."

She just sat there and didn't say anything else.

"Are you here to find out if I want to be on the committee?"

"No."

"Good. After all, this revision is a departmental matter, so it's hard to see how a committee would make any difference one way or the other, right?"

"So you say."

I sighed.

"What's the point of the committee?"

"To propose countermeasures for the course revision, like I said."

I regarded her through squinted eyes and tried to see if I could read anything off her sluggish face. Her hair wasn't in mouse braids today. Instead she had a scarf—in a variety of shades of purple—wrapped around her head. And some dangly beaded earrings, which were also purple. She had obviously put some effort into looking this way. There was something vulnerable and exposed about her attempt, and a little wave of compassion washed over me. Maybe I was being too critical.

"I hear you and Peter are going to Saint Petersburg with Frank," I said, in a tone meant to signal interest and kindness.

Ingvill jumped with a level of vigor I hadn't thought she possessed.

"You know," she said, "I would kindly ask that you refrain from asking me pointed questions and making veiled accusations about conniving!"

"I didn't say anything about conniving! I was just trying to be nice! Besides, I still don't even know why you stopped by my office. Why are you here?"

"You'll find out soon enough."

"Great."

"Fine!"

As she left she made an attempt to slam my office door, but it had a tendency to stick so it just closed on its own with a petulant *humph*.

9

Saturday arrived with autumn sunshine on wet grass, and Bjørnar got up early and made croissants. Late in the morning I sat in the bright sunlight and spread strawberry jam on the freshly baked goods, with the newspaper and a cup of coffee in front of me. The two older kids were lying on the living room floor drawing, and Alva was on the sofa listening to an audiobook.

In this light, our house seemed just fine.

"We can't do it," Bjørnar said, as if echoing my thoughts. He set down the section of the paper he had been reading and looked at me. "It's going to be too expensive, and there could be way too many unwelcome surprises. I'm sure another house will turn up, one that's newer and in a better location. This one is practically downtown, you know. Alva would have to start at a different elementary school than the other two. We just can't do it."

I looked him in the eye and was tempted to tell him I agreed. A new house was risky. It meant being willing to wager everything: the harmony I felt now, the security of everything and everyone being in place, the familiar sounds, knowing the neighbors were pleasant and upstanding people.

The idea of moving was scary. There were no guarantees that it would go well. It could turn out badly, very badly.

What if our family life was all due to our living in this specific house? People often said that remodeling a house could lead to divorce, but what if it was the move itself that ruined things? What if there was something magical about a certain house that allowed a relationship to withstand reality? And if leaving that house meant stepping outside the magical shield?

Besides, Bjørnar was better grounded in reality than I was, and the problems he was pointing out were probably realistic.

But the memory of the house glowing in the darkness was too strong. And I was thinking about how we were going to get old. Not yet, but soon. And then we would need a home. A proper, solid, roomy home.

"Have you noticed how often Ebba sits in the back storage closet?" I asked. "Every afternoon she gets a pillow and squeezes herself down between the shelves in there, with a book or a sketch pad or the iPad. It's the only place in the house where she can be by herself."

"But then she has a place for that, right?"

"Yes, a cramped place without any windows and bad lighting. And Jenny never brings anyone over to play anymore, since there's no room for her and her friends to hang out. That's the way it is here. We're together, all together, all the time. Just us."

"We like being together."

"But it's nice to be able to choose."

He sighed and picked up the newspaper again.

"Fine. But you can go on your own, right? I don't like open houses. You know that."

"We can't make an offer on a house that only I've seen! We're going together. It won't take long, and it's a nice walk. Look at how nice the weather is. We can ride our bikes."

He sighed again, but we ended up taking Alva and biking over to the open house. The two older girls made it clear they didn't want to see any lame house and went off to go hang out with some friends.

As we approached, I started to get butterflies in my stomach. There it sat on the slope, so inviting it almost sparkled. And although I tried not to, I immediately started planning huge Christmas parties that began with the guests stomping snow off their shoes on the steps and walking inside to the aroma of slowly roasted goose and bubbling gravy and juniper and all kinds of other exotic scents and domestic wizardry.

At the same time there was also a quivering uneasiness within me. An uneasiness about the choice that might lie ahead of us. Because this was just the kind of thing that would rouse the Tehomic forces. They had only been dormant this long because I had kept a low profile.

But even more than that, I now realized, I felt an uneasiness about how many people were looking at the house right now and thinking similar thoughts. The young female lifestyle bloggers and nouveau riche oil engineers. Interior architects and café founders. Surely there were people willing to trade in their upmarket Canada Goose winter jackets for a cheaper brand like Bergans or Kari Traa in order to afford this house. Or even worse—there might be people who had enough money to buy the house *and* do any remodeling it might need.

"Why did you sigh?" Bjørnar asked.

"Lifestyle bloggers," I said, lifting Alva out of the bike seat. "I bet a lot of them will show up at the open house. Shabby chic, you know."

"We'll see," he replied and took Alva's hand, "we may not even like it."

I snorted, while little tingles ran up and down my spine at the sight of the big planter pots of blue and lavender hydrangeas lining the walkway to the front door, and the tiles and chandelier in the hallway that were even more beautiful in real life.

We took off our shoes and walked into the living room, where Alva immediately freed herself from Bjørnar's hand and ran over to a bowl of chocolates.

"M&M'S!" she cried excitedly, scooping up a big fistful.

"No, Alva," I warned, "don't take the candy! It's just for decoration!"

"I'll watch her," Bjørnar assured me. "Why don't you go have a look around?"

I nodded and took a few steps toward the dining room, where the real estate agent was. He was talking to an elderly woman who had made herself right at home at the dining table, while another woman stood in the doorway to the kitchen, practically swooning. I noted with relief that neither of them looked like lifestyle bloggers.

"My daughter won't be home for a couple of days," the woman sitting at the table told the real estate agent. "So I wonder if we couldn't set up a private showing on Wednesday?"

"In principle that would be fine," the agent said, "but we've already received a few offers, so the property may already be sold by the end of the day on Monday."

My throat constricted and I tugged on Bjørnar's sleeve as he walked past with Alva, whose face was covered with chocolate and who was pretty much ready to go home.

"Chocolate is yummy," a voice mumbled.

I glanced over and saw that it was the swooning woman, talking to Bjørnar.

"It's the best," he replied and lifted Alva so she could touch the chandelier.

The lady smiled lopsidedly and took a swig

70

from a hip flask that she pulled out of an inside pocket.

"Cough medicine," she explained to me. "I've been a little under the weather lately."

I tried to close my mouth and turned to Bjørnar.

"Should we go take a look upstairs?"

"More M&M'S," Alva whined, pulling on his hand.

"You go," he said. "I'll be up in a minute."

The stairs were soft and uneven and bathed in sunlight and led up to a second story that featured three bedrooms the size otherwise found solely in furniture catalogues.

They had done a great job with the renovation. Bjørnar and I could never have pulled this off. Tasteful wallpaper with birds and stripes, beautiful built-in closets featuring exquisitely made hooks, the original floorboards painted a dark brown, tiny tiles in the bathroom, and a superwide showerhead, the kind I had only ever seen in hotels.

I was standing there admiring it when I heard the stairs creak and Alva's chocolate-covered face appeared atop Bjørnar's shoulders.

"Did you eat all the M&M'S?"

She nodded contentedly. It wasn't until just then that I noticed how shabby she looked. Boots that hadn't been cleaned off after a slushy week at preschool and long underwear covered by a well-worn wool sweater and her raincoat. We should have at least put a clean skirt or a pair of pants on her. The way she looked now, she might as well have been in pajamas.

Not that my own outfit was much to brag about. Old baggy pants with a hole in one knee and a faded gray H&M jacket that was missing two buttons. I also hadn't bothered to wash my hair, just put it up in a limp ponytail.

Shabby minus the chic, that was us.

To be sure, this was also a stroke of genius. It would keep us under the radar.

But I was the only one who knew this.

No wonder the real estate agent hadn't bothered to greet us.

He was surely disappointed, poor guy. It wasn't much of a turnout for an open house: a shill standing in for someone who couldn't come, a wino, and a family of paupers. He was bound to be wondering where all the lifestyle bloggers were. As was I.

"Where's the door to the attic?" I wondered.

"Maybe here?"

Bjørnar pulled on a little closet door, which opened onto a narrow staircase.

I lost my breath. A secret entrance! I was right! This was no normal house. Portals to revelations and insights into another world. Anything could happen here. Maybe it was a blessing? Maybe this actually was a house with an even *stronger* magical shield? An opening to the sun itself?

My heart started pounding again, and I reminded myself that it wasn't by any means certain that it would become ours. *But we were meant to live here,* said another, far more powerful voice. This was a gift. Money? We had money! Why else was Bjørnar working so much? What was the point of being a lawyer if one couldn't live well?

He stood looking out one of the bedroom windows.

"What a view," I commented. "Imagine falling asleep to that."

"These must be the original windows," he said, poking at the frame. "They're going to need replacing, all of them. Can you imagine what that's going to cost?"

"Hmm," I mumbled absentmindedly.

I walked dreamily down the stairs, but when we got to the basement, I realized the competition had picked up. One family in particular stood out. The man's hair was short on the sides and long and slicked back on top. He wore a dark parka and matching slacks, and the woman had a big scarf arranged over a feltlike sweater and tight gray pants. They were accompanied by a kind of miniature version of the mother, topped with blonde curls and a ribbon and wearing a dusty-rose jacket and matching tights. On her feet she wore clean, attractive leather boots.

"There's no room to put the sofa here," Shabby

Chic told her husband. "Can we move the wall?"

He started knocking vigorously on the wall.

"Paneling," he said. "We'll move it. Plus the kitchen would have to be expanded. I think maybe an island in there. And new countertops. Silestone."

She nodded contemplatively, and I threw up into my mouth. Oil money. Most likely an engineer and a graphic designer. They would remove the door hiding the attic stairs. And the portal to the other world would close and the magic shield would vanish. Possibly forever.

In a panic, I turned to Bjørnar, but instead crashed into a young pregnant couple.

"Sorry," I said and laughed slightly, but they didn't seem to have noticed me.

"How practical to have a separate 'children's wing,'" the pregnant lady exclaimed with air quotes.

"Yes, and the kids can use the basement entrance when their friends come to visit," he chimed in.

I snorted. *Children's wing.* This couple would fill the house with ten million books on how to parent. Besides, they were far too young to own a house like this. This wasn't where you moved when you were expecting your first child. You bought a condo or maybe a modernist town house with a cute little yard. Not an enormous, stately old home! And the same goes for the shabby-chic family. What would they use all the space for? Walk-in closets? A wine cellar?

I was seething. Didn't any of these morons get that this was my house? Mine and Bjørnar's and Ebba's and Jenny's and Alva's? Ours!

Suddenly going back home to our actual house felt unbearable, and all the warm fuzzy feelings from a leisurely morning with the newspaper and the croissants were gone.

I was repeating to myself the importance of breathing from the belly when Bjørnar came and took me by the arm.

"Did you get to see everything?"

"Yeah, I think so."

"Then I guess we can go? But put your name on the list."

"Really? You mean it?"

"Yeah, let's put ourselves on the list."

Joy darted through my chest, and I pulled him close and kissed him before we went back to the dining room, where the agent was now talking to Shabby Chic.

Neither the agent nor the woman paid any attention to me, but that didn't matter. We were meant to get this house. We, the Ragamuffin Family, were going to move into this house with its portal to another world. It was meant to be. So all these other people could just go take a hike!

"How high can we go?" I asked Bjørnar as we biked home.

"Not much over the list price. I'll have to crunch a few numbers. But I'm in court all day Monday, so in case it comes to a bidding war, we'll have to agree on a maximum offer in advance. Then you can handle the back-and-forth."

"Marvelous," I rejoiced. "I'll take care of it!"

10

Monday morning I hung up my "Testing in Progress" sign again before I sat down at my desk and pretended to work. When the real estate agent finally called, it was clear that he'd already begun to grow weary of the whole "interested" list.

"Are you considering making an offer?" he asked in a monotone.

"We're thinking about it," I said. "Have you had any other offers, by chance?"

"One. For six point eighty-five million kroner."

"How long do we have to put in an offer?"

"Until noon."

I asked him to contact me if any more offers came in before then, and he called back after just five minutes.

"We received an offer for seven point one million."

"What? *So* much? Are there any others?"

"Yes," the agent responded. "The people who made the first offer are planning to increase their bid. How about you?"

"I'll add fifty thousand," I said.

Then I sent Bjørnar a message: *I offered 7,150,000. We'll see how it goes.*

Our deal was that we would give up and walk away at the list price, which was 7.25 million.

"If we go over that, we'll be struggling," he had concluded after plugging through our budget three times. "Because I haven't set aside all that much for unforeseen expenses. True, it did look like it had been nicely maintained, but at the same time it's almost a hundred years old, so we have to assume that things will pop up."

To my despair, I had scarcely sent the text before someone else added another hundred thousand and then someone put in fifty thousand on top of that. It was a bidding war. I went to the bank's mortgage calculator to find out if maybe we could swing a little more, but it only showed astronomical sums that seemed abstract and unreal and I couldn't really see how these numbers had anything to do with me.

So when the agent called me back, I added another hundred thousand, even though it was over the limit we had agreed on. After all, we wouldn't necessarily need any money for repairs right in the beginning. And Bjørnar was always so cautious. It was up to me to secure our future now.

It kept going like this for a little while longer.

I did some calculations and estimates of my own.

Until everything started to melt together and I could no longer distinguish plus from minus or things that had been said from things that had only been thought.

When the agent called to congratulate me, I wasn't sure what he meant.

"The other bidders hated to withdraw, but they had already offered more than their limits," he said. "So the house is yours now."

I looked down at the piece of paper where I had tried to jot down how much the offers were as we went along. But after 7.5 million, my handwriting became illegible and I appeared to have started drawing hobbits instead.

I wondered if it would be socially acceptable to ask him how much we had ended up agreeing to pay.

Probably not.

"Do you want to discuss the move-in date now, or should we do that at the contract meeting?"

"Could I maybe call you later?"

"Sounds great."

I put my head down on the desk and tried to think.

What was the last offer I remembered making?

Nothing. Apart from the offer that was supposed to have been the very last one, which was 7.25 million. But on my piece of paper it said 7.5 million. That was way too much. And that was also a lot of minutes ago. Many, many, many minutes.

I called the real estate office and gave the man who answered a fake name. I told him I was wondering if the house had been sold and, if so, what it went for.

"I'm not sure," the man replied, "but I can transfer you to the listing agent if you'd like?"

"Oh, no. That won't be necessary," I hurried to say. "Couldn't you just check for me?"

"Sure. Please hold for a moment."

Pause.

"It went for eight point two million kroner."

I concentrated on breathing.

Breathing was incredibly important. The brain needed oxygen to live.

So I breathed in.

And out.

And in.

And out.

I was still practicing breathing when Bjørnar called at noon.

"We're taking a break here now," he reported. "Has the bidding started?"

"Yes."

"What's the price at?"

"It's over."

"It's over?"

"Yes."

"Oh. Well, then, how much did it go for?"

"Eight million two."

"Eight million two!"

He laughed and I could picture him shaking his head.

"Hope the buyers have a lot of money. How many people were bidding?"

"Only three."

"*Three?* How long did you stay in?"

"A long time."

"How long?"

"Until the end."

"All the way until the end?"

"Yes."

"Well, how high was your last offer then?"

I held my breath.

"Are you still there?"

"Yes."

"How much was it?"

"What?"

"Your last offer?"

"Eight million two."

There was silence.

"*We* bought the house?"

"Congratulations?"

"You're kidding me now, right, Ingrid?"

"No."

He hung up, and I started to cry.

Two minutes later he called back.

"I had to step out. What in the world have you done?"

"I don't know? I got caught up in the excitement."

"Do you know what this means?"

"I—"

"It means we have zero money for repairs, zero money for whatever unforeseen expenses there might be, zero money for vacations, and that we're going to have to think long and hard the next time the kids need winter coats or skis or bikes. Have you heard of living beyond your means?"

"Yes?"

"That's what we're going to be doing now!"

"Don't yell."

"I'll yell if I WANT to!"

"OK."

There was silence.

"I have to go," he finally said. "We're starting again in five minutes. You call the bank and explain what you did."

"Couldn't you—"

"No."

"I'll call them. I'm sorry."

There was more silence.

"To be or not to be?" I tried.

"Don't even."

I sat there all day staring at my computer screen without understanding any of what was on there. I went to the real estate site once and looked at the page for the house. A little yellow note in the corner now said "SOLD."

I gulped, and the tears crept out of the corners of my eyes.

At the same time there was a small part of me that couldn't help feeling happy as I looked at the pictures. This was all ours now. Even if we had to live off oatmeal and charity, we were the ones who got to have the yard, the "children's wing," and the attic.

I didn't want to think about how all of this commotion had probably also awakened Tehom.

The main thing was that this was a home, our home, where we would grow old and keep our dentures, each in our own glass. It was marvelous.

It was after six when Bjørnar's car finally pulled into the driveway. The two older kids were using their iPads, while Alva was watching cartoons. I was waiting for him when he walked in the door, but when he saw me, he looked down and waved me away with his hand.

"I'm tired," he said. "I'm not up to talking about this now."

"We don't need to."

"But *what* were you thinking?"

"I don't know. There were so many numbers, and it all happened so fast. I was trying to take notes. And then I tried to do a few calculations on my own . . ."

He shook his head, but didn't say anything.

"I had the thought that we might be able to call the second runners-up and see if they were interested in taking over at their final offer price," I said. "Then we could just make up the difference?"

"Yeah, we might have to do that. I'll have to do some calculations, but I'm beat right now."

"But maybe we could keep it? That would probably be best."

"*You're* probably not actually qualified to evaluate what the best course of action would be."

"No . . . Did everything go all right in court?"

"I had a little trouble concentrating after lunch. What *were* you thinking?"

"I . . ."

"We agreed, right? Didn't we agree?"

"Yeah, but I didn't want someone else to be living in our house! You know? Well, at least not Ms. Shabby Chic. I bet she drives an Audi. Or the 'children's wing' people."

I made my airhead face and added air quotes.

He sighed.

"Do you want a glass of wine?"

"We can't afford wine anymore."

"But we already bought it."

"OK, sure, but let's wait until after the kids go to bed. Right now I want to eat and take a shower. And be alone for a little while."

I thought about saying that you couldn't be alone in this house and that was really part of the problem, but instead I went into the living room where the kids were. Later I noticed that Bjørnar had his math calculations out at the kitchen table, and when we were sitting on the sofa just over an hour later, each with a glass of wine, he gave me a look that showed he was wondering if I might be a little dim, mentally.

"I don't get what you were thinking," he repeated.

"No. What are we going to do?"

"First and foremost we're not going to let you be responsible for *anything*."

I looked away.

"And I can*not* cut back after all."

"What do you mean? At work? Had you been thinking about cutting back your hours at work?"

"I'm just saying that now I can't, whether I want to or not."

"Should we call Ms. Shabby Chic?"

"We'll keep it for one year and see how it goes. And then we can try to sell again if we find that it's too expensive. And hopefully the market doesn't change too much during that time."

I tried to laugh, but all that came out was a small croak.

"But you're going to need to do all the work when it comes to selling this house: the real estate agent, the appraiser, the staging photos, packing, cleaning. Everything. From now on this is your project. I'm going to have to work as much as I possibly can if we're going to be able to afford this. It didn't occur to you that we were going to have to pay for the agent or the closing costs or the title transfer fee, either, did it?"

I shrank and opened my mouth, but he kept talking.

"If you're going to apologize, you can forget it. Just let me know when you've sold this house. That's what I want. And next time, you could stick to the plan we agreed to."

"But we did agree to make an offer."

"For almost a million kroner less than the one you ended up making."

"Luckily I almost never buy new underwear."

"What?"

"The underwear I'm wearing today, I bought it when we were on that BritRail trip fifteen years ago. I saved us some money there, anyway."

"You know, that's not even funny. You've almost bankrupted us. Do you get that?"

I nodded and took a gulp of my wine. It was a little hard to swallow.

"I'm going to bed. I'm exhausted."

"I'm going to bed, too," I said. "Just so you know."

I took a few good swigs from my glass and tried not to listen to the sound of rumbling from the Deep.

11

Bjørnar looked up from the paper with an expression that showed he didn't understand what I was talking about.

"We have to tell the kids we bought a new house," I repeated.

"Oh, yeah, *that,*" he said tiredly. "Be my guest."

But when they looked at me, their faces were way too full of anticipation, as if they expected to hear that we were going to Legoland or they would be getting their own iPhones.

"Your father and I are getting a divorce," I finally said.

I didn't really know what I was thinking. At any rate I never thought they would take me seriously. It was supposed to be kind of a warm-up joke. I mean, it was totally unlikely that we were going to get a divorce, even with my almost bankrupting us. But when I saw Ebba's and Jenny's faces, I realized it had been the wrong thing to say. It was totally wrong.

"What?" exclaimed Ebba, and I could see a faint quiver in her lower lip.

"You're getting a divorce?" Jenny said slowly.

"Are you completely nuts?" Bjørnar asked.

I tried to laugh, but croaking was still the best I could do.

"We are not getting a divorce," Bjørnar explained. "What your insane mother is *trying* to tell you is that she spent absolutely all our money, along with quite a bit of money we don't have, buying that house we went to look at last weekend. So we can't get divorced, because we can't afford it. We're going to move, all of us together. In just a few months."

"Ta-da!" I shouted and flung out my arms. "Then you'll each get to have your own room. How great is that?"

They looked down at the table.

"We're not getting a divorce," I repeated. "That was just a bad joke. Daddy and I love each other very much, right?"

"Right now I love you slightly less than I used to."

"But we usually love each other."

"You're going to have to shape up," he said, setting down his newspaper. "I have to go."

"I don't want to move," Ebba complained. "I want to stay here."

"I totally want to move," Jenny said. "But I don't get where?"

"We're going to move to that red house Daddy and Alva and I went to look at last weekend. The one you guys thought was lame. It'll be wonderful. Right, Alva? Alva?"

"What?" she asked without looking up from the iPad.

"We're going to live in that house with the M&M'S. Isn't that great?"

"I like M&M'S."

"There, you see?" I concluded.

Bjørnar leaned over and gave Ebba a hug.

"I'm sure it will be fine, Ebba, honey. But right now we have to go. I can give you guys a ride. Mama has to drop Alva off at preschool, and then she has to get busy selling the house we live in now. For a lot of money."

"Someone will snatch it up in a flash. *No problemo*!"

I called the real estate agent who had recently sold our neighbor's house.

"Yeah, a lot of people thought that house was too big, so there may be some interest on the market for your property," she said.

"Great," I said. "Maybe you could call some of the people who were interested in the neighbor's house? We'd actually consider selling our place without listing it. The whole process is so exhausting—the photo shoot, all the open houses, flyers, all that business—we'd actually love to skip all that, save a little money, save ourselves a little stress."

The real estate agent chuckled softly.

"There's no way out of it. If you want to sell, you have to take the whole enchilada. But I could come over and take a look—now, actually—and give you an idea of what I think an appealing list price would be and go over my terms. What do you say?"

"Sounds good."

Twenty minutes later both she and her Mulberry bag arrived at the door.

"I would love to sell this house," she said. "Should we sign the papers?"

"I have to discuss it with my husband first."

"Oh, really? I doubt you'll be more satisfied with anyone else. Look, I already filled out the form for you. All you have to do is sign here and here and here."

"Hmm," I said. "We might as well get this ball rolling as soon as possible."

Two hours later, I had signed a contract with the agent and had an agreement for the photographer and the appraiser, and for the next couple of days, everything that happened fell under the header of Selling the House. It was almost like when I became a mother for the first time and the whole world revolved around spit-up and the color of Ebba's poop.

Just a tiny bit more hollow and depressing.

It wasn't until I saw the Filipino au pair sitting at the bus stop that I thought of her and her flood-ravaged family. I made a U-turn and then pulled into the bus stop.

"Hello!" I called out my window. "Would you like a ride?"

She eyed me skeptically, but ultimately nodded.

I leaned over to open the passenger door and simultaneously shoveled a few wadded-up facial tissues and cracker crumbs off the seat.

"Did you get in touch with your family?"

The au pair nodded.

"Yes, they're fine."

"Great news! I'm so glad!"

And that was actually true. Right at the moment I did feel quite happy. The photographer who took pictures of the house earlier in the day thought our house had been "delightfully styled" and concluded, "Good location, well maintained, nice size, and realistic listing price. It'll sell in a flash!"

I squirreled those words away, hiding them inside me like a treasure.

And now the au pair said her family was safe. There were good vibes in the universe. This day was the beginning of something good, a portal to happiness, to selling the house, to a magical shield, to Bjørnar loving me again.

All the fear that had amassed was obviously just silliness. Our buying that house wasn't hubris. Nothing was moving around in the Deep.

The house was a gift.

12

But when the day of the open house arrived and I hadn't showered in three days and my whole life had narrowed to considerations of what to move out and what to leave, how the furniture should be arranged to maximize the feng shui, which cleaning and polishing techniques produced the best shine, and how much money we should invest in flowers, it was hard to distinguish gifts from burdens.

Maybe it was because I walked around in a constant state of low blood sugar or because I'd scarcely slept, but a buzzing had settled in my body. Or a trembling. I felt like I was electric, without knowing how to switch off or how to pull out the plug.

Because everything had to be perfect.

Especially since suddenly, in the last few days, so-called experts had showed up on the radio and TV talking about a residential housing bubble that might burst at any moment. I didn't get where these people came from. But now that they were here, they wouldn't quit talking.

"The worst thing you could do right now," they claimed, "is buy before you sell. And it's going to get worse. I wouldn't be surprised if prices fall by ten to twenty percent."

I'd stopped listening to the radio when I was in the car.

"I wonder if I'm coming down with some kind of heart disease," I'd told my doctor. "I have a lot of chest pain all the time. It's like an iron hand is squeezing my heart. It's hard to breathe. And I can't really stand up straight. I'm sort of hunched over all the time."

"Your blood pressure is fine," she'd said, "but you're low on B12. I'm going to schedule you for injections."

It still felt like I was having a constant heart attack, though. Even when seven people came to the open house.

Because none of them made an offer.

"Why isn't anyone making an offer?" I complained to our agent over the phone. "A lot of people said they were interested."

"The market decides."

"What do you mean by that?"

"There won't be any offers unless the market is interested."

"Is the market interested in other houses?"

"It depends."

"On what?"

"On the market, as I said. It's selective."

"A selective market?"

"Right. You just have to be a bit patient. If this keeps up, we might want to consider lowering the asking price."

I put my head in my hands and sat like that until there was a knock on my office door and Frank poked his head in.

"Doesn't it say 'Testing in Progress' on my door?" I asked, not looking up from the desk.

He closed the door partway to check.

"No. Are you giving an exam right now?"

"No. Come in."

Over the last few weeks Frank had been growing the kind of beard that made him look like he had been raised by wolves. I hadn't been up to commenting on it. He insisted it was his new girlfriend's idea, but no one believed she existed anywhere other than inside his own head.

"I can't really talk now," I told my desktop, "because the testing is actually starting soon. I'm administering some exams for the University of Bergen, via VideoLink."

"I notice that you've been proctoring a lot of exams lately, but that's fine. I'm leaving early today. I'm meeting my girlfriend."

"Great."

"She's from Lillesand."

"I see."

"She's a real estate market analyst."

"Really?"

There was a moment of silence.

"Have you guys sold your house yet?" he finally asked.

"No."

"Wasn't there someone who was going to make an offer?"

"No."

"But you said that, didn't you?"

"She changed her mind."

"Why?"

"Didn't like the tiles in the bathroom."

"Why not?"

"Don't know."

"What's the plan now?"

"The market will decide, but it's selective."

"Are you going to have more open houses?"

"Saturday. Another house on our street is for sale, too. We're going to have a new open house on the same day as theirs."

"Same kind of house?"

"Yup."

"Uh-oh."

I looked at him.

"What did you just say?"

"I said *uh-oh*."

There was that stabbing sensation in my chest, more intense than before. I tried to detect whether any pain was radiating to my arms, because according to the doctor that was a sure sign of a heart attack.

"I have to go," I said. "I'm giving a lecture."

"I thought you said it was an exam?"

"That too."

"Did you hear that I'm going to Russia?"

"Is that where your girlfriend lives?"

"No, she's from Lillesand. Like I said."

"Huh."

"Internationalization."

"What about it?"

"That's why I'm going to Russia."

"Right."

"I was selected to be part of the delegation that's going to look into the feasibility of setting up an exchange program with Saint Petersburg State University. Because of my extensive internationalization expertise."

"I thought Peter and Ingvill were going, too?"

"Yes, but they don't have the same expertise. Peter's coming just because he happens to have been to Russia before, and Ingvill . . . Well, to be honest, I don't really get why she's on the committee at all. She has neither the academic clout nor the background in bilateral exchange agreements."

"Ugh."

"What do you mean by that?"

"I'm just glad I'm not going."

"Not just anyone gets selected to be part of a delegation like this."

"No, obviously. Anyway, I have to get going now."

I hustled Frank out the door and locked it, before jogging down the hall murmuring my silent thanks that at least I wasn't going to Russia.

I was still doing that ten minutes later as I tried to summarize Lacanian ontology in the foul-smelling chemistry lab I'd been assigned to teach in.

"What is real," I stated, "is everything we can't capture in words or thoughts, everything that can't be categorized or explained, like desire or trauma." *Or Tehom,* I thought to myself. "And in Henry James's *The Turn of the Screw*, 'the real' is all the unwritten letters, everything that remains unsaid, all the ghosts."

I could tell they had divided themselves into pretty much two camps. Half the class was tuning out and surfing the Internet on their cell phones, but the other half was on the verge of getting it. And I knew that if I just played my cards right, we could quickly reach the point where on the last day of the semester they would climb up onto their chairs and declaim:

> O Ingrid! My Ingrid! Our fearful trip is
>   done;
> The ship has weather'd every Tehom, the
>   prize we sought is won.

That was my dream scenario, to lead them to an epiphany and then experience a moment of all-encompassing acknowledgment that would bathe the entirety of my pedagogical existence in golden light. Because I was the captain of this ship. And I was leading us all toward the final goal.

Life-altering insight. Fundamental understanding.

So I gave it my all. I drew diagrams and scribbled incomprehensible words on the board and managed to push aside all thoughts of the selective housing market. For a while, it seemed as if Lacan had designed all his incomprehensible theories with Henry James in mind, as if the two of them worked in perfect symbiosis. The one shed light on the other and vice versa. It was like I was burning with fever. I was in the zone and had a continual string of new epiphanies myself. The whole lecture was like one enormous victory lap.

When a student who had never opened his mouth raised his hand toward the end of the class, my joy was complete. Sweaty and exhausted, like a cross-country skier flinging herself over the finish line, I called on him expectantly.

"Yes?"

He eyed me from under his ball cap and waited a moment. I could already hear the words in my head: *O Ingrid! My Ingrid!*

"I think we've had enough of a mindfuck for one day," he finally said.

The room went quiet. *Mindfuck? Did he really just say that?*

I tried to swallow the lump that suddenly

appeared in my throat, feverishly searching for something to say that was funny or would put him in his place. Something that would affirm my captaincy and ensure that at the end of the semester they would still climb up on their chairs.

But there was nothing.

"Fine," I croaked. "Same time next week."

No one made eye contact with me on the way out.

I told Bjørnar about it over dinner.

"What does *mindfuck* mean?" Jenny asked.

"It means messing around with someone's head," I informed her.

"Is that what you do at work?"

"No."

"What do you really do at work?"

"Read books and write about them and teach other people about them."

"Do flies live inside us?" Alva interrupted.

"No," Bjørnar said. "They don't."

"Can I be excused?"

"Yes."

I cleared the table and Bjørnar did the dishes.

"Mindfuck," I complained. "Can you believe he said *mindfuck?* About Jacques Lacan! I am super good at explaining Lacan. I own Lacan! *And* Henry James. I *own* Henry James!"

There was that quivering feeling again. I wished I knew where the off button was.

But it didn't seem like Bjørnar had heard any

of what I had said. He was staring into the sink. I didn't like it when he did that. It might mean he was worried. And if Bjørnar was worried, things were bad. In the realm of what really mattered.

"What are you thinking about?" I asked without really wanting to know the answer.

He didn't respond.

The amplitude of the quivering increased, so much actually that my thighs started vibrating out of control. I held them still.

"Bjørnar," I repeated. "What are you thinking about?"

He looked up, confused.

"Me? Nothing." He paused for a bit. "Erik Thorstvedt."

"The soccer goalie? Why are you thinking about him?"

"Dunno. He just popped into my head."

"How worried are you that we haven't sold the house yet?"

"Not very, but I'm certainly going to be."

"People keep bugging me at work."

"People always bug you at work."

"But they're bugging me more than usual. Plus, I think I have a urinary tract infection. Could you drop a urine sample off at the doctor's office for me tomorrow?"

"You're kidding, right?"

"No. You're driving Alva to preschool, right? And I have an early class. I'm quite sure it's an infection, because I have a backache. Plus I think I might have a fever."

He sighed.

"What about the heart attack?"

"It's there all the time. I've learned to live with that."

I was in the middle of a child-hair-washing operation when I heard Bjørnar's voice from the kitchen.

"Hey, Ingrid, it says on the calendar in here that there's a meeting for the PTA's executive board. Did you remember that?"

"Oh, no! Is that today?"

I rinsed the shampoo off my hands and ran downstairs.

"When does it start?"

"Three minutes ago."

"Argh!"

I yanked the bike keys off the shelf and pedaled down to the school without braking even once. Everyone looked up as I burst through the door.

"Sorry," I said to no one in particular and flopped down into the closest chair. "Sorry, I was in the middle of putting the kids to bed, busy day, logistics and stuff."

The PTA president, Martine, smiled disingenuously.

"Now we have a quorum," she announced. "Everyone's here except the principal, who's sick. Assistant Principal Per Henrik is standing in for him."

Per Henrik nodded, not very enthusiastically, and I tried to give him a look that was meant to show that I knew exactly how he felt.

"The first item of business," Martine continued, "is our national holiday, the 17th of May. We have a representative here from last year's 17th of May committee. She's going to tell us a little about how the festivities were handled in the past and give us some suggestions for areas we can improve on this year."

"It's only November," I objected.

"But it's a children's holiday and the PTA is responsible for the festivities," Martine said.

"And to be clear," the woman from last year's committee said, "the 17th of May celebrations don't just happen by themselves. Last year my whole family *and* my mother-in-law ended up manning the food station because no one would volunteer. We didn't get home until ten p.m. *Ten p.m.!* Even my mother-in-law. Plus, all the sacks for the sack race fell apart after a half hour, and the prizes for the fishing game were all junk that the kids didn't want. Some of them even threw their prizes at the grown-ups. I wouldn't be surprised if some of them are still out on disability from that. Not to mention that I've heard from reliable sources that the best prizes have already been snatched up."

"Who snatched them up?" I asked.

"Other schools. Some of the PTAs are so organized that they started gathering prizes for this year's 17th of May celebrations on May 18 last year. So, well, you can see for yourselves that we're already playing catch-up."

"Huh," I said and leaned over my notepad, where a drawing of a hobbit was beginning to take shape.

An alternate I'd never seen before raised her hand.

"Yes?"

"I'm the alternate representative for the third grade and admittedly I've never attended one of these meetings before, but I have actually done a lot of work with ergonomics, occupational safety, and regulatory compliance in the community. And planning for the 17th of May is all well and good, but I think maybe it's an even bigger problem that the children at this school are not receiving enough help tying their shoes."

"Why don't we discuss that when we get to the 'other items of business' line on the agenda?" Martine suggested. "Because I promised—"

"What I'd like to pin down is what type of measures the school is planning to implement," the alternate interrupted, "and at the same time discuss whether the PTA board ought to have responded to the situation sooner."

Everyone looked over at Assistant Principal Per Henrik.

"Well," he said, "are you thinking about shoe tying in general?"

"Yes, actually I am. In general *and* in specific. My son, for example, does not get any help tying his shoes. And do you know what his teacher said? That we should buy him shoes with Velcro closures because the school doesn't have the 'capacity' to tie the children's shoes."

"Yes, ahem," said Martine. "I would've thought that maybe—"

"Ca-pa-ci-ty," the alternate repeated, glaring at the assistant principal.

"Well, it *is* true," Per Henrik explained, "that we encourage parents to teach children to tie their own shoes before they begin school. But Velcro is a good alternative if the child hasn't mastered the skill."

"What did you say?" the alternate asked.

"If the child hasn't mastered the skill of tying his own shoes."

"Are you suggesting that he can't do it?"

"You just said that he can't do it," Martine said with a smile.

"This is nothing to smile about!" the alternate yelled. "This is an admission of failure on the school's part!"

A box of candies was slowly making its way around the table, but at the word *failure* it

104

stopped. I closed my eyes and tried to brace myself for what was about to come.

And what was about to come was a comprehensive list of the pet peeves each individual PTA representative was harboring, everything from how much snow was permissible on the approach to the school before it needed to be shoveled or plowed to how unreasonable it was that the fourth grade was allowed to use the soccer field only once a week. There was so much to discuss that we probably could have kept going for hours and days if the alternate hadn't finally blown her top and demanded that someone from the administration "take charge of the shoelace issue."

"But all you need to do is teach him to—" began Per Henrik.

"I'm going to see to it that your refusal to accept responsibility for this situation is recorded in the minutes," she growled, "and then I demand that someone contact the city!"

"I suppose that's possible," Martine said. "Off the top of my head I don't recall who our liaison with the city is."

The secretary started flipping back and forth through the minutes until she found the list.

"It's . . . Winter? Ingrid Winter?" she reported as if asking a question.

"That's me," I said. "But I don't recall being city liaison."

"Great!" Martine exclaimed, relieved. "Then you'll take the ball on this."

"Uh, what ball?"

"The shoelace-tying issue. We'll put that on the agenda for the next meeting."

"Perhaps we can just include it under 'other matters of business,'" Per Henrik suggested tentatively, "because we probably ought to avoid turning it into its own separate issue."

The alternate snorted and crossed her arms defiantly.

"Hush it up, sure," she said in a huff.

"No," protested Per Henrik. "I'm not hushing anything up, but it's important that—"

"What kind of person are you, anyway?" she interrupted. "And why are you even here to begin with?"

"What do you mean?"

"Is the whole school entitled to be represented at these meetings? I thought this was the parent-teacher executive committee. Not really something for the administration, you see? And you don't even have any children at this school, do you?"

"No, I'm here in my capacity as—"

"Then I think maybe we ought to take a vote on whether or not we think it's a good idea to have you sitting here telling us what to do, telling us that the well-being of our children somehow isn't the responsibility of the PTA."

"But I didn't—"

"Can I see a show of hands? All those in *favor?*"

"I think maybe as president I should—" Martine began, but the alternate stopped her by raising her hand.

"I repeat: all those in favor of parents looking after their children's interests, raise your hands *now.*"

Although many of the representatives took this opportunity to stare at the table, just barely a majority were still feeling the uneasiness from the use of the expression *admission of failure,* which ten seconds later resulted in the alternate watching in triumph as the assistant principal packed up his things and stepped out into the hallway.

"But you can't go home," Martine called out as he walked out, "because someone has to let us out the main door when we're done."

He nodded without saying anything.

"Great," said the alternate. "Now we can relax a little."

This led to the airing of frustrations with the quality of school lunches and how much homework the kids were getting. The alternate also took this opportunity to share her general observations on employment, local government, *and* the lack of follow-up from the on-site after-school day care program with regard to her own child. The planning for the 17th of May was postponed to the next meeting.

When we emerged into the hallway, Per Henrik was sitting on the floor typing something on his phone. He didn't look up when we went by.

Biking home, I pedaled so hard I could taste blood in my mouth.

13

"You can't expect me to deliver this to the doctor's office," Bjørnar said the next morning.

"But I don't have anything else!"

"You want me to walk into the doctor's office with a sample of my wife's urine in a glass that says *Taste the Fjords*?"

"I sterilized it," I said tiredly.

He shook his head and picked up Alva's boots.

"Come on, honey, it's time for us to go."

"I'm so stressed out."

"*You're* stressed out? Is it tiring working in the ivory tower?"

"No, it's all the other stuff."

"You're stressed, I'm stressed, everyone is stressed. Say *bye-bye* to Mommy."

"Bye-bye, Mommy."

"Bye-bye, sweetie!"

I stood by the window and watched them drive away. Five minutes later I pushed Ebba and Jenny out the door and watched them disappear down the street as well, before I headed off to work, planning to finish my conference paper. About Tehom. About Tehom as an all-inclusive chaos-cosmos.

Cosmic chaos.

Chaotic cosmicity.

Tehomic cosmic chaosism.

Silent Tehom that comes disguised as a gift, but annihilates everything.

I sat in the car thinking about how one of the signs of imminent doom was that the contrast between Monday morning and Friday afternoon had been erased. Friday afternoon used to be the best part of the week. That was when Bjørnar and I made pizza and split a beer while we played music and danced and enjoyed ourselves in the kitchen.

Not anymore.

It was as if all that good energy had been redirected somewhere else now. We were still there, all five of us, but now Bjørnar stood in the kitchen alone and made the food like an automaton. I scrubbed the bathroom floor and made the tiles shine, just as much an automaton. Even the children were completely silent, sitting there staring at the TV screen.

I knew why. Fridays no longer kicked off a weekend of freedom and cheerful leisure but rather chaotic cleaning drives and heavy frustration. Lately Saturdays had been spent having open houses, and on Sundays Bjørnar went to work with the same worn-out expression on his face that he'd had all fall. We weren't human anymore, more like zombies, trapped in a world that was dominated and controlled by the Dictator of Housing Sales.

In this new reality, Monday morning was almost preferable. It was almost a relief to go to work and hear knocking on the door. It was a blessing to know there was another universe populated by humans who didn't care about the downturn in the housing market and who didn't hold conversations in which this premise lurked under everything.

"Yes," I called.

"I found a solution," Peter said with a wink, "the perfect solution, you might say."

I was still wondering if he had intended to wink or if it was maybe a nervous tic when I realized he was waiting for me to respond.

"To . . . ?"

"I know how we're going to reverse the planned course revision!"

He swept into my office and started waving around the folder he had tucked under his arm. It reminded me of the one we'd received from our real estate agent. I felt nauseated and opened my mouth to lie and tell him I had an appointment and couldn't talk, but wasn't able to get anything out before he flopped down on the chair and opened the folder. Inside there was a single sheet of paper with some scribbles on it.

"I have a friend in the private sector," he said with satisfaction, "and he tipped me off to a negotiation strategy designed to outmaneuver the other party."

"In the private sector?"

"Look," he continued, "we're meeting with the administration next week, right? We're going to suggest a plan for how we envision the new course offerings and how these are going to fit into the new overall BA and MA programs, right?"

I nodded slowly.

"Well, my strategy is that we show up at the meeting without a plan. Wait, please don't interrupt me. *We* have no plan, we say. *They're* the ones who have to propose a plan. And when they do, we counter them with the following tactic. Because we actually do have a plan—namely for this revision never to take place. Do you have a red pen?"

I passed him a red pen and he motioned me closer.

"So, here's what we do."

I found myself looking at something that resembled the kind of play diagram a soccer coach might show the players before a big game. Under my name it said "bad cop."

"Bad cop," I read, and glanced up. "What's that?"

Peter smiled.

"According to my sources, a bad cop behaves in an aggressive, antagonistic manner. In other words she opposes every argument put forward by the other party, and actively works to suss out their weaknesses."

"I see?"

"Yeah, and then eventually brings the whole negotiation to a standstill, but we'll cross that bridge when we get to it."

I looked down at the diagram again.

"And you have Frank listed as . . ."

"Frank is the good cop. That doesn't really need any explanation, and actually we don't even need to tell Frank about this at all. Good cop is his normal modus operandi, if you will, so that's kind of the path of least resistance."

"Ingvill, then. She's the hard-liner?"

"Right. She'll stall for time and make sure our team keeps its focus."

"You think that's a good role for Ingvill, do you?"

"It's not ideal. I'll concede that, but there wasn't anyone else left after I put myself down as leader. So Ingvill will be the hard-liner. She really wants to do it and is going to practice. Did you know she has a personal trainer? He's going to help her with the psychological preparations."

I kept looking at his diagram without saying anything.

"Is bad cop the same as fall guy?" I finally asked.

"What do you mean?"

"I get that we're all on the same team, of course, but to me it looks like the bad cop is the most inflammatory of the roles, and I would assume that the one who's always objecting to everything and being difficult isn't going to get all that much sympathy from the administration and could pretty quickly end up being the one who finds herself reorganized into the preschool-teacher education program. If you're actually right that that's the real purpose of the course revision plan."

He laughed a little too loudly and ran his hand down my arm.

"You don't think I'd do something like that to you, do you?"

"Maybe not, but then I don't get why I can't be the hard-liner and Ingvill could be the bad cop."

He pulled his hand through his hair.

"That's how I had it! But then I talked to her first. She threatened to put me out on a leave of absence if I listed her as the bad cop, so then I had to amend the diagram. Sorry."

He sighed heavily and made puppy-dog eyes at me. I sighed at least as heavily.

"I can't promise anything," I finally said.

"Marvelous," he replied and circled my name. "Marvelous. I knew I could count on you."

Then he disappeared out the door, leaving me with my thoughts.

I considered going to the chair to inform her that Peter was losing his marbles, but didn't really have the energy for that. Besides, I had to write that paper on Tehom for the conference and save my energy to form a protective shield around the children and make the phone ring with the news that somebody wanted to buy our house."

But first of all I was going to the break room to make myself a cup of coffee. We didn't have any left at home, and I hadn't been able to face buying more. But as I walked down the hall, I felt like my head was getting too much oxygen. I shook it to try to let some of the air out, without success. It was like walking on a ship in a raging storm, and I saw the floor rising toward me. I clung to the wall.

Someone took me by the arm.

"What's wrong?" asked the chair.

"Dizzy."

"Have a seat."

She pulled me into her office and pushed me down onto an uncomfortable chair that had probably been manufactured to encourage whoever sat there to get up and leave as soon as possible.

"I'm going to call your husband," she said. "What's his number?"

I enunciated what I thought his number was.

"He's on his way," she informed me a moment later. "I have to go to a meeting with the dean, but you can just sit here until your husband gets here. If you have to throw up, I recommend you do it in this trash can."

"I don't think I'm going to throw up."

"No, but I think we'll put it right here, anyway. Take a sick day tomorrow."

I nodded.

"Fine," she said and gave me a firm pat on the shoulder.

She was hardly out the door when I started vomiting. It came out like a projectile and landed in the trash can with a splash. Then it happened again. The third time, I could hear people swarming in the hallway.

"Is someone not feeling well?" I heard them wondering.

"I think it's Hildegunn," another chimed in, and an instant later at least three people burst in on me at the same time.

"Hi." I smiled wanly. "It's just me. I've got a little touch of something, but my husband is coming to pick me up, so it'll be fine."

"Does Hildegunn know you're in here?" a woman from the Religious Studies Department asked, her face skeptical.

"Yes."

"Oh, really?"

I could feel her eyes on me until she and the others abruptly withdrew and shut the door. Out in the hallway people were clearly still gathering.

"What's going on?"

"I thought I heard someone being sick."

"Is Hildegunn sick?"

"Relax," the religion lady said loudly. I could picture her holding up her hands to ward off all the comments. "It's not Hildegunn. It's only that . . . What's her name again?"

Several people suggested names.

"Nygaard?"

"Larsen?"

"Andersen?"

"No . . . the other one . . . Winter! It's her."

Someone mumbled, "Oh, right." And then I heard feet shuffling away and doors closing along the whole length of the hallway, and I closed my eyes. I could have been dead and none of them would have cared.

But Bjørnar cared. He drove me straight to the doctor, who stated that this was what happened when you didn't eat enough meat and developed a B12 deficiency.

"I don't eat meat," I mumbled with my eyes closed, "because of the turtles."

"What?"

"She said she doesn't eat meat because of the turtles," Bjørnar repeated.

"What?"

"We visited a turtle hospital last summer," he explained, and I noticed that he sounded tired. "And she saw one of them being operated on and it looked so much like a human that she decided to become a vegetarian."

"It looked like my grandmother," I added.

"What?"

"It looked like her grandmother."

"OK, but grandmother or not, you have to make sure you're getting enough vitamins. Do you want to feel like this for the rest of your life?"

"No."

"Then you have to eat meat. And we'll step up your B12 treatments."

Bjørnar got me home and into bed, and when I woke up the next morning, he was sitting on the edge of the bed watching me.

"Every morning is gray," he said.

"I know that."

"It didn't used to be like that."

"No."

"I'm scared it's always going to be like this."

"Yes."

"You need to pull yourself together. All these . . . quirks of yours. You can't always live them out so intensely. When you start buying houses for eight million kroner and walk around talking about heart attacks and urinary tract infections and stress cancer and have dizzy spells—then it's not OK anymore. You have to think about the kids. And about us as a family. Everything is revolving a little too much around you right now."

"Yes."

"I'm going to work now. And I won't be home until late. I'm preparing for a trial."

"OK, have a good day. And sorry."

He got up and walked out of the room. I thought about calling out, "To be or not to be," but it didn't feel like I had permission. Besides, I wasn't up to it. And I certainly wasn't up to getting out of bed and taking care of the kids. I wished the doctor had admitted me to the hospital and not just sent me home again. If only she could have given me morphine or anesthesia or something that would let me lie totally still in bed and sleep. Or put me in a coma. Just for a few days or a couple of weeks. Until all this was over.

14

Saturday morning Bjørnar took the kids to the library, while I stayed home to get the house ready for yet another open house.

The doorbell rang twenty minutes too early. I was still squatting over the mop bucket. I cursed private showings in general and mopping in particular and then stashed the bucket behind the washing machine and opened the door with my widest smile.

But it wasn't the people for the showing.

It was a man, scruffy and odd, with long, greasy hair and wearing the world's widest tie. He stood there smiling back at me. I realized right away that he could easily be a serial killer, and decided not to let him in under any circumstances.

"*Tjenare*," he said, greeting me in Swedish. "Or hello."

"Are you here for the open house?" I asked.

"Yes . . . maybe?"

"Either you are or you're not."

"It's a nice house. But maybe it's missing something?"

He took a few steps toward me, and I clutched the doorknob harder. I didn't like this. He had crazy eyes. Plus he was Swedish.

"What do you mean?"

"Do you have an alarm?"

"No."

"Fabulous! Then I can cut you an amazingly good deal. It's so good that, strictly speaking, I'm not allowed to go this low. But we're making a few exceptions only in your neighborhood, for people like you."

"I'm not interested."

"Let me ask you this: How many pairs of shoes do you own?"

I didn't answer right away, trying to remember where I'd put my cell phone. Wasn't there a serial killer who had collected his victims' shoes? Jerry Brudos?

"One," I lied.

"You only have *one* pair of shoes?"

"Give or take."

"My point exactly, give or take."

"What *is* your point exactly?"

"Most people simply don't know how much they own. May I come in?"

"No."

"It would be easier."

He put his foot on the threshold. I held on to the doorknob even tighter, ready to close it.

"Do you have children?"

His breath smelled like cigarettes. I pictured his black lungs, with scarcely any openings for the oxygen, decaying a little more each day from the toxins. I wondered if he knew that cigarettes contain a substance that numbs your throat so you don't feel how much it hurts when you inhale the smoke.

"I have children, yes."

"How old are they?"

"They're . . ." I took a breath and plucked up my courage. "You know, now's not a good time. Perhaps you could come back another time?"

"They all say that," he said, sounding irritated. "Well, let me just jot down your name and phone number, because this is an offer you're not going to want to miss!"

"Actually there's no point in your calling, because we're selling the house. I'm actually having an open house now, so it's as good as sold. You'll have to talk to the new owners."

He laughed and shook his head.

"You haven't sold it yet. We'll just see how that goes."

"What do you mean by that?"

"You've heard of the housing market crash, right?"

He made an explosion sound with his mouth and illustrated with his hands everything being blown to smithereens.

"I hope for your sake that you haven't bought a new place yet."

"I have to go," I said and tried to shut the door, but his foot was in the way.

"What's your name?" he asked.

"It's . . . Anne Undheim," I told him.

"Uh-huh. And your phone number?"

I made up one of those as well.

"Great. I strongly recommend that you get an alarm system. You know what happens when someone breaks into your home? They don't just steal, you know. They make a mess and ruin your stuff. They urinate on your walls. They stick your toothbrushes into unmentionable orifices."

"What?"

He winked at me.

"You can avoid all that with an alarm system. I'll give you a call on Monday! But then I'll expect to come inside. It's really outrageous to be left standing outside like this!"

He gave me a slightly accusatory look and only slowly removed his foot. Once his foot was out of the way, I pushed the door shut with all my might and hurriedly locked it. My heart was racing. I had survived, but only just.

The people for the open house didn't arrive until a good while after the appointed time. I had planned a few choice remarks about unpleasant Swedish alarm salesmen, but opening the door, I became distracted by how tall they were. They were so tall that I actually suspected them of being replicants. Especially since the male looked suspiciously like Rutger Hauer, and the female had a particularly meticulous hairdo that

I had only ever seen in ads. Her short black hair stood straight up in a sort of a swoop to the left, which until I saw it I would have doubted was even possible to pull off in real life.

"Welcome," I said, compensating for my lack of height and my limp hair by squeezing their hands extra hard during my handshake.

"Thank you," they said and removed their shoes.

Despite their potential replicant status, I was happy to see that they were my age. Plus they both had steady jobs in the financial sector, so surely they also had actual money. The last private showings had been to two young couples currently renting basement apartments who should have been touring a "spiffy town house with sunny patio."

All I had to remember in order to land this was that replicants weren't the easiest to communicate with. Because their memories had been implanted, not experienced firsthand, it was hard for them to understand the emotional aspects of human life. Irony also wasn't their forte.

But beyond a doubt they were equipped with an interest in interior design, because I could hear them talking about knocking down walls, building a loft, and putting in recessed lighting. They stood for a long while debating the purpose of the owl decals that adorned Alva's bedroom wall. They concluded that they'd been put there to spruce up the space and give it the feel of a child's bedroom. They also agreed the owls could probably be removed.

Easy peasy, I thought.

"Are you guys always so tidy?" she asked as they came back downstairs.

"We like to keep the place clean," I said. "It gives us peace of mind."

"But surely not as clean as this?"

"No, maybe not exactly *this* clean, but it's not so far off."

She stared at me as if she were trying to read my mind.

"I hardly believe that," she finally concluded.

"Suit yourself."

"Who put the owls on the wall?"

"I did."

"I don't like owls. Can they be removed?"

"Of course."

"Can you prove that?"

"They're decals. They come off."

"Can you prove that?"

She stood and watched while I tried to remove one of the owls without damaging the paint. The hard edges of the decal cut in under my fingernails, but I held on to a straight face. When I was done, she ran her hand over the wall.

"No damage, right? No marks that I can see, anyway."

She moved her head slightly and I chose to

interpret that as a faint nod. Standing like that, she actually reminded me of an owl herself.

"Do you have any children?" I asked.

They exchanged glances, as if they didn't understand my question.

"Children aren't compatible with our lifestyle," Rutger Hauer finally said.

"We've never considered it," she added.

"Would you like to take a look at the outside?"

"Could we see how the gas fireplace works?" he asked.

I picked up the remote control and turned it on.

"Can't you make the flames any bigger?"

"Yes."

I opened the panel and turned up the dial that controlled the heat.

"Is that the highest?"

"Yes."

"You can't get it any higher?"

"No."

"Can you see the flames from the yard?"

"When you're sitting on the patio?" I asked confusedly.

"Yes."

"I don't know. I've never tried."

"Let's do that now, then," Rutger Hauer said.

"Sure."

They went outside, and I opened the panel and turned the heat all the way up. I peered out at the two of them standing side by side in the yard. It was hard to tell if they were satisfied or not, so I gave them the thumbs-up with a questioning look. They made a vague hand gesture that could mean anything from "very nice" to "far below average." Maybe they were replicant models that didn't come with the hand-gesture package preinstalled, or maybe they had not had much of an introduction to empathy.

I was crying as I walked downtown to the library, but luckily it was raining. In response to Bjørnar's question about whether it had gone well, I told him they were replicants, which made it hard to relate to them and also made them impossible to read.

"Remind me what replicants are again?"

"Humanlike cyborgs with implanted memories, who can only be detected with questions that elicit their fundamental lack of empathy."

"And the movie we're talking about is . . . ?"

"*Blade Runner*."

"Exactly. And you think they're replicants because . . . ?"

"I guess they just gave me a replicant vibe."

He nodded and was quiet for a minute, and I hoped his silence meant that things were looking up between us and that he didn't think it mattered that I thought they were humanlike cyborgs.

"Are replicants allowed to own property?" he asked.

"I don't know," I said, "but I kind of hope so."

I didn't mention my suspicions to the real estate agent, but just said I thought the showing had gone well. When she called them, though, they denied having ever seen the place and said they weren't interested in buying a house, anyway.

"Strange," she said.

"Manufacturing glitch," I said.

15

The following Monday the chair of the department summoned me to the meeting room.

"I'm going to be honest with you," she said after I sat down in the same chair I'd been placed in the week before. "I hear you're planning a mutiny, and I don't like it."

"Pardon me?"

She pulled out a sheet of paper with some scribbling on it.

"Do you deny writing this?"

"No. I mean . . . yes."

"I've been informed that you're the one behind this document," she said, tapping her finger on the sheet of paper accusingly as she watched me expectantly.

"That's incorrect."

"Is it also incorrect that you're going to play 'bad cop' at the meeting when we discuss the course revision? Is it also incorrect that Frank is going to play 'good cop'?"

"Listen—"

"I think you're the one who should be listening to me now."

She leaned over her desk, took off her glasses, and looked me right in the eyes.

"How are things going on the home front?"

"Good, I—"

"You went to see the doctor about your dizzy spell?"

"Yes, I—"

"I've heard you're trying to sell your house. Is it not selling?"

"No, but—"

"We couldn't sell ours when we tried, either, the one on Lysegata. It was on the market for six months. I thought I was going to lose my mind. We lost an unbelievable amount of money on that, but we got back on our feet again."

"It's really hard," I admitted. "And I—"

"My point, Ingrid, is that you can't take out hostility you're feeling—at the housing market or real estate agents or nonexistent home buyers—on your coworkers here. Documents like this"—she waved Peter's piece of paper around— "aren't constructive. The course revision is being imposed on us by the college. It's not my place or your place or the place of any of the others in the department to agitate."

I tried to get a word in edgewise, but she just brushed me aside.

"Cooperation, Ingrid, is the key. Not activities that undermine this institution."

"No," I said tiredly. "No, I do understand that."

"And Ingvill as 'hard-liner'? What were you

thinking? She can't stay focused for five minutes! And Peter as 'leader'? Honestly."

She laughed heartily and slowly ripped the piece of paper into little pieces.

"I think we'll just forget this whole business," she continued, "put it behind us. I won't bring it up with the dean. You're selling your house, you're tired. It's understandable. But this is unacceptable."

"I'll—"

"You'll take over the local coordination work for the revision."

"Me? But that's the faculty coordinator's job."

"The faculty coordinator has enough to do. Anna has three kids and a husband who works in the private sector. We can't saddle her with this. I'll make sure you get the notes she's taken so far. This is a time-consuming process with a ton of meetings and possibly some overtime. But not paid overtime. You should be prepared for that. Teamwork, Ingrid. Maybe it's time you learn a little about that."

"But I have three kids, too. And a husband who works around the clock. In the private sector. It's not feasible for me to put in overtime. Especially now that we're in the middle of selling the house. The house we bought cost—"

"Maybe you should have thought about that before, Ms. Bad Cop. And then maybe you should have . . . um, what was that again . . . ?"

She started flipping through her notebook.

"Maybe you should have 'mindfucked' your students a little less."

"What?"

"There have been complaints. The students claim that you're messing around with their heads, confusing them, not imparting the reading-list material in an intelligible manner, and spending all your time on movies and pop culture."

"I was teaching Lacan. And Henry James. It's complicated material. We were using *The Matrix* as an example."

"No need to get into the details. Just stick to the syllabus. Got it?"

"Got it."

I wanted to say something more, but didn't really know what, so I pushed the chair back, got up, left the room, and started the trek back to my own office while trying to pin down the crux of what had just happened.

My cell phone rang.

"Hello."

"*Tjenare*," a monotone voice greeted me in Swedish. "I'm calling for Anne Undheim."

"Who?"

"She gave me a phone number that doesn't seem to be correct. I met her at your home address. This is about the property at 32 Pine Lane. We had agreed that she was going to buy an alarm system, but I haven't been able to reach her."

My heart was pounding hard in my chest, and I realized I had to lie. Again.

"Oh, Anne Undheim, yes," I said. "She doesn't live there. She was only there to clean."

"Are you the home owner?"

"Yes, but we don't want an alarm system. The house actually sold. We're moving tomorrow."

"Do you know what happens when someone breaks into a home—"

"I'm just heading into a tunnel," I interrupted. "So I can't quite hear—"

I hung up. Two seconds later he called back, but I rejected the call and then turned off my phone.

A little butterfly-like sense of mastery fluttered in my chest for a second before I spotted Peter's back disappearing around a corner farther down the hallway.

"Peter!" I yelled. "Peter, wait!"

Any idiot could see that he sped up, but it didn't matter, because I soon caught up with him.

"Peter," I said, taking him by the arm. "I know you heard me, you Judas. You need to tell the chair that I wasn't the one who wrote up the good cop/bad cop plan."

"Why?"

"Because she thinks I'm planning a coup, that's why!"

"Ah," Peter exclaimed, beaming, "that's perfect!"

"No, that is not perfect! Because now I have to take over coordinating the course revision, and that means a ton of extra work and meetings and stuff I don't have time for! Plus, I'm already in trouble because of the awful job I did as faculty coordinator. Not to mention mindfucking my students."

"I don't know anything about the mindfucking, but I thought you were great as the faculty coordinator."

"You're the only one, then."

"Well, to be honest, it's good she thinks you're the one behind it, because then I can proceed undisturbed. That's why we leaked your name."

"What do you mean?"

"It was Ingvill's idea. She can be quite brilliant."

"Ingvill," I muttered.

"What was that?"

"Do you realize what you've done? This was surely Ingvill's plan all along. Now I'm the fall guy. You see? Just like I said!"

"Oh, you're exaggerating. After all, you were the faculty coordinator until just recently. You know the administration, and they know you. You're safe. If anyone from here is going to be exiled to the preschool-education program, it's not you."

"But they thought I was a bad faculty coordinator," I hissed.

He smiled and patted my shoulder. I sighed heavily.

"Fine, I won't say anything. But could you please knock it off with the hard-liner plans? I'll do my best to secure our interests. And I'll try to make sure no one gets sent to the preschool program, no one other than Ingvill. What do you say?"

"We'll see," Peter responded evasively. "We'll see."

"Promise me!" I called after him, but he just raised his hand as a kind of good-bye.

On my way out of the office, I saw that the chair had called. But I had no intention of calling her back.

16

Unfortunately there was already another course revision meeting the following day. The administration was meeting with the chair, a representative from the applied pedagogy program, and the ergonomics, occupational safety, and regulatory compliance officer. Frank immediately sidled up to the latter and tried to talk his way into getting an adjustable-height desk.

"That's not why we're here, Frank," the chair said.

"As the ergonomics, occupational safety, and regulatory compliance officer, I'm always on duty," the officer objected, thoughtfully twisting his mustache.

"Exactly," said Frank, lowering one shoulder and stretching his back so they could tell how much he was suffering from not being able to raise the height of his desk. "The university needs to take care of its employees' needs when they arise."

"I want one of those adjustable-height desks, too," Ingvill demanded.

She was wearing her hair up with a bunch of flower-covered hair clips and looked even crazier than usual, sort of a hybrid between a six-year-old and a sixty-year-old, like Bette Davis in *What Ever Happened to Baby Jane?* or like tropical-fruit salad in human form.

"What are you talking about?" the chair protested. "You already have one, don't you?"

"What?"

"You got one of those desks when you started going to physiotherapy two years ago. I remember quite clearly, because we set it up the day before I left on my maternity leave."

Ingvill looked confused, and I wondered if this might be one of her hard-liner tactics, dragging the process out no matter what, even if it made her seem crazy.

The ergonomics, occupational safety, and regulatory compliance guy was rummaging around in a stack of paperwork, and I took that opportunity to make eye contact with Peter. I raised my eyebrows to check if we were still following the game plan or if we were abandoning it, but he just gestured that he had no idea what my eyebrows were trying to say.

"Well, at any rate that's not the subject of today's meeting," the chair said. "So . . ."

The ergonomics guy cleared his throat and raised two fingers to indicate he wanted to say something.

"You're right," he confirmed. "Ingvill already has an adjustable-height desk."

Then Frank exploded.

"I can't believe *she* got an adjustable-height desk when I have a very obvious back injury as a result of—"

"Fine," the chair said. "Fine, fine, fine. We'll send you to occupational health and then we'll take it from there. Good?"

Frank raised his hands to show that in a pinch this course of action could be considered "passable," but that there was no way it could be characterized as "good."

"Good," the chair said. "Then let's get down to business. The reason we're here is to discuss the course revision, and perhaps Ingrid could tell us a little about how the work is coming."

"Yes." I nodded. "I didn't have much of a chance to prepare, but I have reviewed all our course offerings and at a minimum I can say that we're going to have to cut out two undergraduate courses. So, I suggest we get rid of Lexicology with Didactics. That class has been unpopular with students for a long time, and the material could easily be integrated elsewhere. As for the second class, I suggest World Lit. It's popular, but we can't get rid of any of the other literature classes. This is the only class we have that's not introductory."

I looked around the table for nods of approval or smiles. As far as I could tell, this solution was a little stroke of genius, since it didn't result in any redundancies or across-the-board modifications.

But the meeting table was surrounded by poker faces.

The chair was poking intently at her iPad and hardly seemed to have heard what I said. The only one who nodded was the ergonomics, occupational safety, and regulatory compliance officer, but since he was staring straight at the wall, it seemed more like he was having some kind of attack.

I was opening my mouth to add a comment about how great my suggestion was and at the same time introduce the plans for the graduate level, when a note was plunked down hard in front of me. It said, "BAD COP!!!" I glanced up and found Ingvill, Frank, and Peter all glaring at me. Peter even started nodding his head demonstratively toward the administration.

I shook my head.

"No," I whispered. "No!"

All three nodded vigorously, and Ingvill made some motion with her hand that clearly depicted decapitation. Was she threatening my life?

"Was there anything else, Ingrid?" wondered the chair.

"No, I . . ."

I had thought out what I was going to say. I was going to present my whole solution and explain how it ensured full workloads for everyone in the department while at the same time benefiting the students, but I couldn't stop looking at Ingvill, who had proceeded to plunge an imaginary knife into her stomach while pointing at me.

My phone also started vibrating on the table in front of me right then, and when I glanced at the display, I saw that it was the Swedish serial killer.

I gulped and glanced down at the sheet of paper where I had meticulously written out all the details about how we could do this efficiently and without costs. Then I took a deep breath.

"I want one of those adjustable-height desks, too," I said.

"What?"

"Yeah, if everyone else is getting one, I want one, too, one of those adjustable-height desks. I've been having some back pain, you see. Quite a bit of back pain, actually."

The chair of the department pushed her chair back, regarding me with a look that was at least as stony as the ones I'd received from the rest of my colleagues a few seconds earlier.

"So you want a special desk," she repeated slowly.

"Yup."

"How about a special *chair,* then? Would you like one of those?"

I cleared my throat inaudibly.

"Yes," I confirmed. "Maybe so."

"One of those chairs with no back support?"

Her eyes were narrow and confrontational. Out of the corner of my eye, I could just barely see Ingvill smiling triumphantly in the background.

"Dunno," I said quietly and then gulped.

"I want a chair," Peter interjected. "One of those special chairs."

"Me, too," Frank chimed in.

"Me, three," Ingvill said before adding, "well, another one."

A complete silence fell over the room. The chair jotted something down on a piece of paper before raising her head and giving me a look. It was a look that said I was about five minutes away from being reassigned to the preschool-teacher education program and the only thing that could save me now was a complete course reversal.

Teamwork, I thought to myself, *teamwork.*

I don't remember much of what happened after that, but I'm quite sure I was the one who started pounding my fist on the table. Up and down my fists moved, first softly and then harder and harder. Eventually I started chanting, first quietly and then louder and louder.

"Desk, desk, desk, desk, desk, DESK, DESK, DESK."

Everyone joined in. Louder and louder we repeated our demand until the word *desk* lost its meaning and was transformed into an absurd demand that surged through the room in protest and anger.

"DESK, DESK, DESK, DESK!"

"FINE!"

The chair stood up and leaned over the table, assessing us with a dragon-like expression that was actually quite scary.

"Don't think that I don't know what you're up to. But I can play that game, too. This meeting is adjourned. I'll call another one, and next time the dean will be here, too. Maybe even the university president."

"The university president?" Ingvill said meekly.

"That's right. And you know how he feels about this department and the subjects you all teach. He's no *fan*. Let's just put it that way."

"Is including him really necessary?" Peter asked hoarsely.

"It is," the chair said. "It is."

We all got up, but the chair didn't move. She stood there, leaning over the table.

"Ingrid, stick around for a minute," she instructed without looking at me.

I desperately tried to catch Peter's eye, but as usual all I saw was his back as he hightailed it out of the room.

Meanwhile, the chair indicated that I should take a seat closer to her, then sat down and studied my face.

"I am particularly disappointed in you, Ingrid,"

she finally said. "And I think now would be a good time for you to stop and reflect, really stop and reflect. Thoroughly. Give a little thought to how you want to spend the next twenty years and what you want to be doing. Research? Or teaching 'Old MacDonald' on the guitar? It's your call. Luckily there's a place where you can take some time to reflect."

"There is?"

She nodded slowly.

"Uh, where?"

"Russia."

"Russia?"

"We're trying to reach a cooperative agreement with Saint Petersburg State University. I'm sure you've been following that."

"I—"

"As I'm sure you know, the university's motto is *innovation*. But we also support internationalization, and especially with an eye to the east. So we're sending a delegation to spend a week at the state university."

"But the delegation has already been selected, right? I thought Frank—"

"That's right: Frank, Ingvill, and Peter. Three people. The Russians prefer three-person delegations. They don't like two. And certainly not four."

"But there are already three people going, right?"

"But it's two men and one woman. That's no good."

"The Russians don't like men?"

"They like men, but we don't. Two men and one woman doesn't look good. It sends mixed signals about where we stand on gender-equality issues. That's why I've decided Frank will stay home. You're taking his place."

"But I'm going to a conference in a month, and—"

"And next week you're going to Russia."

She looked at me over her reading glasses.

"In Russia they don't look lightly on things like 'mindfucking' or this whole 'bad-cop' mentality. Nor do they have adjustable-height desks or special chairs. So, I want you to go there and do a little reflecting, give a little thought to what *I* want. And what I want right now is good feedback about networking progress, synergistic internationalization, and bilateral cooperation. You got it?"

"Got it. But I—"

"Good. That will be all."

In my head I tried to figure out if there was any way at all to get out of this, but it was like I was having an out-of-body experience. As if the desk demand had created a chasm inside me that couldn't be crossed, by myself or anyone else. So I stood up and took a few steps toward the door.

"Oh, by the way, you need a visa to travel to Russia," the chair said without looking up. "I suggest you go to Oslo this week and get that taken care of. I'm sure they must have some kind of same-day expedited visa application. Good luck!"

17

"Russia?" Bjørnar repeated, as if he hadn't really been clear that such a place existed.

"The worst place on earth," I said. "But I have no choice, not after the desk fiasco. If I don't go, I'm going to end up teaching preschool. And you don't need to remind me that it's only a few weeks until we move, and that there are a thousand things to be done. Packing, cleaning, potential private showings, and we have to get ahold of a big truck to haul some stuff to the dump."

My voice broke and I glanced up at him. He stared at the wall behind me, looking like he was still wondering what Russia even was or just how low we were going to sink into financial and emotional ruin. The thought made my thighs start trembling, something which had gradually come to be my new normal.

"We'll have to hope I don't get the visa," I said.

"Have to hope," he repeated, like a lethargic parrot, "have to hope."

And I was still repeating it to myself three days later as I stood shivering outside the closed Russian embassy. A lady in a pink down jacket hurried past me, down the little walkway that led to the entrance, opened the door, and disappeared into the building. A few minutes later a man in a black leather jacket arrived and did the same thing. Even though it said in bold all-caps on the embassy's Web page that it did not open until nine o'clock and that NO ONE should even consider approaching the door before that time.

There was absolutely no point in standing there in the autumnal darkness like some fool. So I, too, slowly made my way down the walkway and cautiously opened the heavy front door, which turned out to lead into a small brown waiting room predominantly furnished with plastic chairs and empty water jugs. Even though there was still half an hour to go before they opened, there were already groups of people by the bulletproof windows, babbling away in Russian into the microphones mounted on the wall. I also noticed that all the written information was in the Cyrillic alphabet, including whatever it said on the enormous take-a-number machine in the middle of the room.

"Hello, Hal," I mumbled stiffly to the machine.

Indecipherable letters blinked at me above a square clearly meant for entering numbers.

I entered my confirmation code.

No reaction.

My phone number.

No reaction.

Passport number.

No reaction.

1-2-3-4-5-6.

When I entered that, an alarm started going off, which caused everyone to turn around. I desperately entered more numbers, until a door opened at the other end of the room and a large woman with a fluffy perm pushed me out of the way, unplugged the machine, and then plugged it in again.

"Never enter random numbers," she scolded and disappeared back to where she'd come from.

"I don't understand what I'm supposed to do," I called after her. "I can't read Russian!"

"Birthday," another man in a black leather jacket, who had just entered the room to the accompaniment of the hysterical alarm, informed me. Trembling, I entered the six numbers in question and in response received a ticket on which it said "113." A moment later it was magically my turn, even though there were at least fifteen Russians slurping coffee while they waited in the randomly placed plastic chairs all over the room.

Meanwhile, my sense of accomplishment was dampened by the man behind the window who exhibited zero interest in acknowledging the physical manifestation of number 113. Instead, he sat gesturing to a young man in a glossy mafia suit, whom I'd seen smoking out on the front walkway ten minutes earlier. The two were clearly disagreeing about something. Mafia Suit explained something at length, while my guy alternated between frenetically shaking his head and resting it in his hands.

I thought two things. The first was that Mafia Suit was basically crocodile food. My guy's black hair came from a bottle and he was definitely from the Soviet era, while Mafia Suit looked like he was born in the nineties and probably didn't even know there was a pit of crocodiles waiting under the floor. He was likely under the impression that the world he'd been born into was full of perestroika and possibility.

The second was that their disagreement might soon boil over onto me. Even though I didn't want the visa—like, at all—I also knew that coming back empty-handed would instantly demote me to teaching preschool. Plus, I estimated the chances that I, too, was standing over a trapdoor to be well over 50 percent, so Mafia Suit and I would probably end up being crocodile food together.

Thus, I was ready with my biggest smile and my most positive vibrations when Mafia Suit stomped off in frustration and Hair Dye slowly turned toward number 113.

"Hi!" I hollered into the speaker in my most chipper voice, waving to the window. "*Privyet!*"

Hair Dye showed no sign of having seen or heard me, but used a weary hand motion to indicate that any paperwork should be placed in the metal compartment. I obediently inserted my passport, certificate of valid travel insurance, the invitation letter issued by Saint Petersburg State University, and my fully filled-out application form and barely managed to yank my fingers free before he pulled the compartment back to his side of the window with a sharp metallic bang.

I regretted not having followed my doctor's admonitions to eat better: more meat, more vegetables, more of everything. It was probably my inadequate diet that was making me feel so light-headed and weird. Sometimes the dizziness followed me into my dreams.

"Five days," I suddenly heard the speaker announce in a crackling bark.

It startled me.

"Excuse me?"

"The visa takes five days. One, two, three, four, five."

"That won't work. I'm *leaving* in five days. One, two, three—"

He cut me short with a shrug.

"But I read about something online called an expedited visa. That's what I want."

"There's no such thing."

"Yes, there is. It says so right here."

I pulled out the printout I'd brought with me.

"See, right here? If I pay six hundred kroner, I

can get it same day. It says so right here. This is from your Web page."

With an irritated look, he held up his hand: five fingers.

"But the expedited visa—"

"Doesn't exist!"

"I have money. See? Six hundred kroner in cash. Just like it says online."

I held up my bills and smiled hopefully.

"*You* decide?"

"No. But online it—"

He slammed his fist down on his desk so hard that everything on it bounced into the air.

"MOSCOW decides! Not the Internet!"

"But—"

Clang!

The metal drawer popped out containing a receipt. Then Hair Dye moved his finger to a red button on the left side of his desk. He pushed it hard and I closed my eyes and held my breath, waiting for the trapdoor to the crocodile pit to open. Instead, the man in the black leather jacket tapped on my shoulder and shook his head as if to say nothing could be done.

"You're not in Norway now," Leather Jacket said. "Now in Russia."

"Right," I said, proceeding slowly toward the exit, but Hair Dye stopped me, barking something in Russian while thumping one hand on his bulletproof glass and indicating with the other hand that I was an idiot.

"Take the receipt to the cashier," Leather Jacket explained.

I peered around looking for anything that might resemble a cash register and eventually chose the window with the most Post-It notes on the glass, where the brusque lady handed me a new receipt.

"I don't want a visa," I said, waving the receipt. "Can I get my passport back instead?"

"Five days."

"But I don't want to go to Russia! I've changed my mind."

"Five days," she repeated, shaking her head to indicate that I would indeed be going. "You go."

A gesture that was repeated by the chair of the department when I told her about my problems.

"You can change your ticket. Take a later flight and go via Oslo. You're going to Russia, and you're going to set up a cooperation agreement. Simple as that."

Even Bjørnar shook his head at me, but that was because he was laughing, in a way I hadn't seen him laugh for a long time. It gave me hope. Maybe I should go to Russia, if for nothing else than at least getting some good stories out of it, stories that could save my marriage, even though I had plunged us into financial ruin.

"But I'm scared of ending up in one of those little cages they have in their courtrooms."

"You're scared of a lot of things," he said. "If you go to Russia, you might actually get so scared that your fear flips and reverses direction."

"You mean, like, it might ease up some?"

"Maybe."

I lay in bed and mulled that over. The thought of going to Russia caused an iron fist to squeeze my heart like never before, and my scalp itched so much I was sure I must have lice. But at the same time Bjørnar had put an idea in my head. Maybe this *was* a good thing? Maybe I just needed to be more scared than I'd ever been before. Maybe that would help me develop some kind of superpower.

18

I tried my all-out best to avoid Frank, who I knew must be awfully disappointed about losing his chance to internationalize, but the day before I left he succeeded in tracking me down.

"You weaseled your way onto the committee," he said resentfully.

"I didn't weasel my way onto anything. I—"

"*No one* knows as much about bilateral cooperation as I do. No one!"

"That's probably debatable, but the point is that I don't even *want* to go. But I have to. In part because of this whole bad-cop strategy that—"

He interrupted me by holding one finger up right in front of my nose and glaring at me.

"You see this?"

"Yes."

"Does it stink?"

"Not particularly."

"That's weird, because I think something smells fishy here, very fishy!"

I sighed.

"Look, I wish you could go in my place, but it's not up to me. And if you're going to blame anyone, you should be looking at Peter and Ingvill. They're the ones who started this whole bad-cop strategy. You know that, right?"

"VERY FISHY," Frank roared into my face, then spun around and marched down the hallway.

"So I'm going," I told Bjørnar that same evening.

"Yes, I'm aware of that."

We stood there, surrounded by cardboard boxes.

Not that we ever talked about them. We'd stopped talking about anything that had to do with houses or our home life. Which is why neither of us mentioned that I would be coming back shortly before our move.

Even though we were nowhere near selling the current house.

Even though neither of us remembered why we'd even wanted to move or why we'd gone and bought that enormous old house that we'd only been inside once and could hardly remember in the first place.

Not to mention that lately I'd started realizing that most of the families in Astrid Lindgren's books weren't actually all that happy. I mean, come to think of it, you really only found those wonderful Christmases in the books set on Troublemaker Street and in Noisy Village. Other than that she mostly wrote about kids who were parentless. Or their mothers were working themselves to death and their fathers were alcoholics.

So I was a little puzzled about what I'd actually been thinking.

Meanwhile I was going to Russia.

"Bye," I said, waiting for some kind of well wishes from Bjørnar or maybe something I could draw strength from.

"Bye," he said.

I swallowed the lump in my throat and walked into a different darkness.

A Tehomic darkness I would descend down into and maybe learn how to manage. Deep, deep down.

But there was one bright spot. Since I'd changed my tickets so late, I also had to upgrade to first class. And first class meant one thing: champagne.

Not to celebrate, I told myself. *But because I can. So chill out, Tehom!*

I practiced my drink order several times to myself, but ended up hoodwinked by the man next to me.

"Coffee and a macaroon, thanks," he said.

"Coffee and a macaroon, thanks," I repeated.

A macaroon? I didn't even like those. Not to mention that obviously an airplane macaroon wouldn't even be a normal macaroon but something goopy and soggy, like congealed palm oil.

Still, things went really well for a while. The coffee was nice and hot. I had a book to read. There was no turbulence.

Then things started going downhill. First, it turned out to be the wrong book. A child is sent to loveless foster parents in Wales while his parents end up in a concentration camp? My tears were dripping into my coffee cup and all over the pages of the book, and I started to notice the trembling in my head again.

I inhaled quickly and realized the palm oil nugget had settled in my stomach like a lump. I had to get off this plane—now!

I looked at my watch, which showed that there were almost two hours left until we arrived in Saint Petersburg.

I tried to pull myself together, but my mind went blank.

What was happening to me?

I had always had these sorts of tendencies.

But I'd also always had some degree of control over them. When the anxiety was there, it was usually more like a hum, kind of like unliberated negative potential.

Not this time.

I wondered if maybe this was the turning point. People who are crazy haven't always been crazy. They didn't need to be institutionalized their whole lives. But eventually you snap.

And become psychotic.

I felt the iron fist tighten, and looked down at my thighs.

I couldn't be on this plane anymore.

It was untenable.

What if I never got out?

This seat.

The curtains separating us from the common masses in economy class.

The little window.

The clouds outside.

The iron fist.

I considered looking for Peter and Ingvill. I hadn't seen them, but knew they were aboard somewhere. I quickly pushed that thought aside. They would probably just make everything worse.

I looked over at the macaroon man next to me.

I gulped.

"Hi," I said, trying to look friendly. "So, what brings you to Saint Petersburg? Business or pleasure?"

He looked up from his in-flight magazine in surprise.

"Business," he replied tersely.

"Oh, I see," I said, focusing everything I had on my next question. "Me, too. What do you do?"

He hesitated a little.

"I work for the Kongsberg Group."

"Ohhh," I said, trying to keep from screaming.

Did they keep straitjackets on planes? I had to avoid losing it. I tried to think of something I could ask Mr. Kongsberg about.

"How exciting," I said enthusiastically. "Is that a big company?"

He looked taken aback.

"You haven't heard of the Kongsberg Group?"

I shook my head.

"Oh. It's one of the biggest companies in Norway. We have seventy-five hundred employees."

"Wow, that's a lot. What do you do for them?"

"I'm in charge of their weapons systems group."

"I see," I mumbled. "I see. Like for hunting and fishing?"

"Not exactly."

"No?"

"No."

"War?" I asked and laughed loudly.

"Defense systems."

"Right, defense systems, of course."

Now would be a really good time for me to wrap up this conversation, but the iron fist was still squeezing. And I felt like I was hyperventilating. If only I could faint.

"And what about in your spare time?"

"Uh, why are you so interested?"

"Oh, no reason. Long flight. Nice to chat. Get acquainted. With new people. It's normal."

"I'd prefer to read, if you don't have any objections."

"No! Being well read is the foundation of culture."

I laughed again, way too loud, and on top of

that gave him two thumbs-up, but Mr. Kongsberg didn't see that, because he'd already turned back to his in-flight magazine. And so I, too, bent over my book, which was now just a smear of ink and wet splotches. I pushed the button as hard as I could to call the flight attendant. Multiple times.

"Could I please have some wine?"

"Of course," she said. "What kind of wine would you like?"

"Red," I said. "No, wait. White. No, wait. Red *and* white. And champagne."

"We only have prosecco."

"Prosecco is fine."

Two minutes later she returned with the bottles, which I emptied in record time. In reverse order. And the last thought that crept into my mind before I fell asleep was that resolving a panic attack with alcohol definitely marked a new step toward the bottom.

19

It was clear the woman in the passport-control booth wasn't particularly eager to let me into the country, and I wondered if that was because I seemed drunk or because I didn't seem drunk enough. Still, my visa obviously checked out, so she didn't really have any grounds to deny me entry. All I could hope now was that the return trip would go just as smoothly.

I shared that thought with Peter and Ingvill when I met them at the baggage claim carousel.

"What do you mean?" Ingvill asked.

Peter scoffed.

"I'd just like to see them try! I'm a British citizen. Still, I get your point, Ingrid. The whole system is reactionary after all."

"Are you talking about gay rights?"

He waved me off.

"Everything happening here in the Soviet Union is part of the same ideological battle that has gone on for ages."

"Uh, I think it's called Russia now?"

He scoffed again.

"Really, Ingrid, you can be so naive! Do you really think the Russian Bear ever planned to put up with the structural fragmentation that took place in the nineties? Open your eyes! There's every indication that the Bear is waking up, and at the end of the story, there will be a new, and possibly even stronger, Soviet Union. Mark my words. They don't have anything to gain from holding political prisoners at the moment, so we ought to be pretty safe in any case."

Ingvill nodded frenetically.

"After all, we're here to promote academic cooperation with the state university," she reminded us. "Internationalization and bilateral ties. That's the only thing we need to think about."

I studied her. She'd obviously dolled herself up for the trip, settling on a tropical-fruit-salad-meets-Captain-Hook theme. She had something that looked like peacock feathers dangling from her ears and wore her hair up with a heap of bobby pins that were jutting out all over the place. The rest of her outfit consisted of black pirate boots, blue tights, a purple cape-like sweater, and a yellow Gore-Tex jacket.

For his part, Peter had gone with an English lord-of-the-manor theme with brown corduroys, tartan dress shirt, green V-neck sweater, and the kind of traditional oilskin coat you might see a duke trout fishing in. In his hand he held a wool herringbone deerstalker cap.

I had selected exclusively black clothes, for obvious reasons. Ebba had walked in the evening before as I was laying out my clothes on the bed.

"Is that what you're going to wear?"

"Yup. Does it look OK?"

"Mm. You always wear black when you have to do something you're nervous about."

I thought back to when she was in preschool.

"She empathizes with other people's feelings so much," her teacher had explained. "She's always trying to comfort the other children. Sometimes we're almost concerned that it's a little too much."

I felt the tears coming, and I tried to concentrate on the luggage that was now rotating by on the carousel in front of us. I also caught myself wondering if she could see us now, would the chair be satisfied with her delegation?

Luckily our group perked up even more when we met our representative from Saint Petersburg State University. Ivan Abarnikovitch had long, thin hair that was pulled into a ponytail and wore acid-washed jeans and a kind of snowboarding jacket with a leather collar that said "Surf's Up" in big letters across the chest.

Peter, who clearly wanted to distinguish himself as an urbane sophisticate, walked right up to Ivan and kissed him on both cheeks with a passion that seemed to confuse even the Russian. Ingvill and I each received our kiss on the hand, without knowing for sure if this was the norm in Russia or if it was a response to the intensity of Peter's greeting. Ingvill blushed anyway and then snorted awkwardly. That kiss on the hand might be the only bodily contact she'd had so far this year.

Which was probably also why she insisted on leading the way, next to her new Russian friend, while Peter and I brought up the rear.

"Who actually is this Ivan guy?" I asked.

"I'm not entirely sure," Peter replied. "The chair said he was the one who contacted us, not vice versa. Norway's been trying for years, you know, to set up some form of collaboration with the state university without success. So we were surprised when they suddenly showed some interest."

"Is he a historian?"

"No, a philosophy professor. Analytical philosophy, I think."

"Wittgenstein?"

"No idea."

In the car we found out that Ivan preferred to work with Heidegger.

"I've done quite a bit of work on Heidegger as well," I explained. "In my dissertation, for example. Loads of Heidegger. 'The turn' or, well, *die Kehre* as I'm sure you know it, Logos, Being—the whole shebang. I'm studying Tehom from a literary criticism perspective, and it's interesting how Heidegger's concept of *Dasein* helps to illuminate that."

Ivan didn't respond, but said something to

Ingvill, who was sitting in the front seat because she claimed the back made her carsick. I couldn't hear what he said, but it was obviously something amusing, because they both giggled about it for a long time.

I looked out the window. We were just passing a gigantic statue of Lenin. Vladimir looked like he was running at full speed. Probably rushing off to communize something.

"What kind of building was that behind the Lenin statue?" I asked.

No answer.

I repeated the question.

"Please don't bother me while I'm driving," Ivan chided. "There's a lot of traffic. I need to focus."

He kept chatting with Ingvill. I turned to look out the window again.

"Is that Nevsky Prospect?" Peter asked, aiming his question generally at the front seat.

"No," said Ivan.

"Oh, I see," said Peter. "It's quite cold out, isn't it? On the plane they said it was only fifteen degrees! Good thing I brought my coat."

"This isn't cold."

"It feels a *little* chilly," Peter insisted.

"Not cold."

"Fine."

After a while we drove over a river.

"Is this the Neva?" Peter asked. "I've been so

looking forward to seeing the Neva. *Tossing and turning like a sick man in his troubled bed.* Isn't that how the Pushkin poem goes?"

"No," Ivan said. "Not poem. Not Neva."

At that, Peter finally gave up. The two of us in the back seat sat looking out our windows. The two in front kept chatting and giggling.

They actually giggled so much that thirty minutes later when we had to say good-bye to our thin-haired Russian guide, Ingvill looked as if it were the end of the world. She did light up again, however, when she realized that he would be coming back in a few hours to take us to dinner.

For my part I was just immensely relieved that it hadn't occurred to the university that they could ask us to share rooms, so as the others entered the elevator I hurriedly said good-bye and headed off to look for the stairs.

My room was on the fourth floor and was large and turquoise and had a double bed, a chaise longue, a desk, and some big mirrors that looked like the ones you would find in an interrogation room. I lay down on the bed with my head turned toward the windows and watched heavy snowflakes drift down toward the gray canal, the gray cars, and the gray pavement. Even though it was well below freezing the snow didn't seem to be sticking. It swirled into random drifts, piling up near the walls of buildings, railings, or other obstacles but didn't settle on the ground the way normal snow does. This was busy snow. Or some distinctively Russian variety. Matrix snow.

I should shower.

I should call home.

I should work.

Instead I lay there idly following the journey of the snowflakes with my eyes.

20

A few hours later we stood in the lobby again waiting for Ivan. Ingvill had poked a few more bobby pins into her hair, applied bright-pink lipstick, and put on a felted wool dress with a big heart on the chest. Peter had gotten out his tweed suit in addition to wearing something that resembled a cowboy hat on his head.

"Was that in your suitcase?" I asked, impressed.

"Indeed it was," he said. "In its own box. It's an urban bowler. Pretty stylish, wouldn't you agree?"

"Yes," I said. "Very nice."

A second later, Ivan walked up with three paper bags in hand, but stopped short at the sight of Peter.

"Cowboy hat no good," he said.

"It's an urban bowler."

"Like a cowboy."

"No, like an urban—"

"Like a cowboy!"

"This is a neutral menswear hat," Peter objected and looked to me. "Don't you agree? Not something you would wear out on the prairie, so to speak."

He chuckled at the image.

"Well, it does look a little like a cowboy hat," I reluctantly conceded.

"It's not a cowboy hat," Peter hissed.

"Peter," Ingvill said, "if Ivan doesn't want you to wear the cowboy hat, I think we should respect that. If we want to establish a mutually respectful relationship, we need to be sensitive to cultural differences. OK?"

"Fine," muttered Peter with a quiet *hmph*.

"Here," said Ivan and handed each of us a bag.

"What is it?"

"Present."

I peeked into my bag, which contained a box of mints, a map of the city, and a bottle. Could it be vodka? The thought turned my stomach. The only time I'd ever drunk vodka was at a family reunion for Bjørnar's family in Østfold. They didn't serve any alcohol until well into the evening, and when it finally came, there was only cognac or vodka to choose between. The last thing I remembered was Bjørnar throwing up into a plastic bag containing a copy of Dante's *Inferno* and a Sony Sports Walkman, while I threw up all over the bed in the guest room at his aunt's house.

"Peripheral neuropathy," I whispered to a miffed Peter as we walked to the restaurant ten minutes later.

"What's that?"

"It's a fairly widespread problem in Russia, because of the high rate of vodka consumption. It damages the peripheral nervous system and

169

people can lose sensation in their hands or feet."

"Sounds about right."

"I don't like Ivan."

"Me, either."

"But we probably should have brought him a gift," I said. "Maybe we could pay for his meal at the restaurant?"

"I don't care," said Peter. "My head is cold. My urban bowler was specially designed for cold weather."

And it was cold out, no doubt about it. The snowflakes continued to fall from the sky, and there was hardly anyone out and about. Just us. A group of people who didn't actually know each other and didn't want to get to know each other, either, but who had to be together because some PR adviser had come up with words like *internationalization*.

Innovation.

Synergy.

Cold.

Death.

Luckily the restaurant was surprisingly warm and cozy. It was situated in multiple rooms that you entered via hallways and little doorways in what appeared to be a converted apartment or maybe even multiple apartments that had been combined. We sat down at a low coffee table, the kind you would have found in most homes in the seventies, which was surrounded by a big sofa with matching armchairs to further emphasize the hominess.

"What a nice place," I told Ivan.

He nodded noncommittally.

"Irina chose it."

That was when I realized the young woman who had been standing motionless next to the dumbwaiter was with us.

"Hi," I said, holding out my hand. "I'm Ingrid."

She laid her hand limply in mine.

"Irina," she said.

"Are you a philosophy professor as well?"

"No."

"What are you working on?"

"Aesthetics."

"Oh, I see. What kind of aesthetics?"

"Regular aesthetics."

"Literary studies?"

"No."

"Art?"

"No."

Menus were passed around, and Peter took the opportunity to order something to drink.

"Let's celebrate our arrival with a pint," he said. "Perhaps someone could recommend a good Russian beer?"

"There are no good Russian beers," said Irina. "We have no tradition of that."

"But there must be some good Russian beer?"

"No."

"All right." He flipped a little aimlessly through the menu. "Then I'll have a McEwan's. What about you guys?"

"I'll take a McEwan's as well," I said.

"What about you, Ivan Abarnikovitch?" asked Irina.

I saw Ingvill give Irina a sharp look.

"I'm not drinking," Ivan said. "I have to drive."

"Can't you take the subway home?" I asked. "I read that Saint Petersburg has a really extensive subway system."

"I can't take the subway," Ivan said, "because I have to drive you guys around early tomorrow morning. So I can't take the metro, can't drink."

"Oh, yeah," I said. "I see."

Ivan gave me a look that indicated he strongly doubted that I understood anything at all, but didn't say anything.

We moved on to our menus.

"A lot of things on here look good," I said.

Irina snickered.

"There is no good Russian food," she said. "We have no tradition of that."

"But maybe you could recommend something, anyway?" Peter said. "I, too, come from a country not known for its food culture, but it still has its bright spots here and there." He was already on his third beer and looked reasonably satisfied.

"No."

"What about you, Ivan Abarnikonovitch?" Ingvill asked.

"Abarnikovitch," Irina corrected.

"I can recommend the mushroom soup," said Ivan.

"Are you going to order that?" Ingvill asked.

"No."

"What are you going to get?" I asked.

"Nothing."

He lurched into a lengthy explanation in Russian to Irina and gestured for her to explain the gist to us.

"Ivan Abarnikovitch says that he is following strict diet that requires that he not eat anything after six p.m. on weekdays."

"Doctor's orders," Peter said with a wink.

"No."

"Does the diet require you to eat some particular kind of food?" I asked.

"No."

"Just that you not eat after six p.m.?"

He seemed annoyed and waved his hands around even more and said a bunch of stuff in Russian to Irina.

"Ivan Abarnikovitch says that he is done talking about his diet."

"Oh."

I bent over my menu again and ordered borscht and red-beet salad. Ingvill chose a dish called *pelmeni*, while Ivan sat sipping from his water glass.

"What are you going to have, Peter?"

"I'd really like to let our hostess decide."

"Irina?"

"Right."

Irina looked confused.

"You just order what you want."

"But surely there's some specialty that you would recommend? Something I *must* try?"

"It depends on what you like."

"But I want you to—"

"He'll have the borscht," I told the waiter.

After we ordered we lapsed into silence, and I took the opportunity to pull out my cell phone. I'd sent a message to Bjørnar earlier, but as far as I could tell, I hadn't received a response yet. There didn't seem to be any coverage here, either. The hotel claimed to have Wi-Fi, but I hadn't been able to get it to work. I suppose it made sense that there was no contact between the outside world and this snow globe we found ourselves in, if you wanted to look at it that way.

My sensation of being in a snow globe was so strong that it was actually a little hard to believe that Bjørnar and the kids even existed, as if I were a replicant and they were an implanted memory. Maybe this was what hell was. Finding out that you were actually something totally different. That there was no response to "to be or

174

not to be." That it was all just a sequence taken from someone else's life. Or from a TV show.

Because who knew where the replicants got their memories from these days.

The evening ended with Ivan tasking Irina with taking us back to the hotel.

"Couldn't you brighten our journey with your presence, Ivan Abarnikonovitch?" pleaded Ingvill.

"Abarnikovitch," Irina corrected for the fourth or fifth time.

"No," Ivan said brusquely. "I have to—"

"Yeah, yeah," I said. "Drive us around tomorrow."

I felt four eyes glaring back at me, but was too tired to care.

"Well," Peter said. "We look forward to being in your charge again tomorrow."

Once we were back in front of the hotel, Peter turned to Irina.

"Farewell," he said and kissed her hand. "We shall meet again."

"In thunder, lightning, or rain," I muttered.

Then our Russian comrade disappeared into the snow flurries without a word, while we walked just as quietly into the lobby.

21

That breakfast is the most important meal of the day was a fact apparently lost on Ingvill and Peter. They furthermore seemed to be solidly in the majority in this, because there weren't very many guests who'd bothered to make the trip down to the dining room. Aside from me there was only one man in a shiny red shirt and a young couple compulsively holding hands over the table.

When I saw the buffet, I understood why there were so few guests. It appeared to be a mixture of continental and Russian food, and the only thing it all had in common was that it seemed well past the expiration date. The European contributions consisted of something baguette-like, a few slices of cheese with a greenish sheen, a couple of cookies, and a small bowl of muesli. The Russian portion consisted of some kind of porridge and potato pancakes.

I slowly chewed on the baguette, feeling it disintegrate and form an extra layer in my mouth, while the cheese immediately fell apart into small, hard crumbles that I washed down with a few gulps of fruit punch. The man in the red shirt, clearly on a different type of diet, had helped himself exclusively to sparkling wine.

The couple persisted in their heavy petting activities.

Neither Ingvill nor Peter had come down yet by the time Ivan showed up in the lobby, and we ended up having to get one of the front-desk workers to call them.

"They overslept," one of the amazons behind the counter informed us with an impeccable smile.

Ivan groaned and ran his hand through his hair, looking like he wanted to punch someone. Luckily he lit up considerably when Ingvill stepped out of the elevator a few minutes later.

"Good morning, my lovely," he said and kissed her hand.

She giggled and looked at me, as if she were expecting a similar greeting from me. But I was speechless. Her hair was braided like Pippi Longstocking and accompanied by a wide-necked, floral blouse and pants that were a mishmash of zippers and pockets and what looked like parachute cords. On her feet she wore high-heeled ankle boots, which made her twice my height.

Pippi Longstocking meets Bride of Frankenstein, I thought, noting that the baguette and cheese had settled like rocks in my stomach.

"Do we have time for breakfast?" asked Peter, who was dressed for a manorial pheasant hunt. "I have low blood sugar."

"No," Ivan said tersely.

"Maybe we could stop somewhere on the way," I suggested helpfully, "and buy a little food that Peter and Ingvill can eat in the car?"

"No," said Ivan. "No food in the car."

"But . . ."

"Didn't you hear what he said?" hissed Ingvill, leaning over me from her great height. "No food in the car!"

"The breakfast wasn't that good," I said to comfort a pale Peter as we climbed into the back seat five minutes later.

"Maybe they have a vending machine at the university," he muttered.

They did, but when Peter tried to insert coins into the machine, Ivan took him by the arm and led him firmly onward.

"The dean is waiting," he informed us.

Shortly thereafter we stood squashed into a kind of antechamber, where three secretaries were doing their respective best to stack papers, type on a manual typewriter, and open the window. In the midst of all this, Ivan was trying to make our presence known, something which ultimately resulted in two of the secretaries each starting to flip frantically through their appointment books while the third shook her head just as frantically.

After a moderately large dose of roaring, Ivan

stormed out of the room with Ingvill hot on his heels. Peter and I lingered uncertainly, until he bowed understatedly to the secretaries and led me out into the corridor, where we could see Ivan's and Ingvill's backs in the distance.

"Come," growled Ivan.

We followed. Down some stairs and up some stairs and through doors and narrow and wide hallways and past groups of students and employees and old women who looked like they'd just found themselves a bench for the day. Ivan gave us a sort of tour, frantically opening doors to seemingly random rooms, his behavior not unlike that of the secretaries.

"Here," he said as he opened the door of something that looked like a library.

"The library," I said, nodding in recognition. "Wonderful."

He scoffed and waved us on.

Eventually I started having a hard time making informed-sounding comments.

"Ah," I said stupidly, "microphones."

In the end we found ourselves in Ivan's office, where he picked up a phone and started screaming into it.

"Is everything all right?" I asked when he hung up.

"That was my secretary," Ivan complained, irritated. "She's stuck in traffic on the highway, typical woman. I'll chew her out later."

"Why is it typical of a woman to be stuck in traffic?" I asked.

"I'm sure you know," Ingvill said.

She'd sidled in and now stood behind Ivan, rubbing his shoulders. I tried to catch Peter's eye so that we could exchange knowing glances, but he was just sitting there staring at his own knees. He did perk up, though, when some other people appeared. First in the door was a muscular man with short blond hair and light-blue eyes, wearing a turtleneck wool sweater and short dress pants. At the sight of him Ivan jumped up and started to bow, but changed his mind halfway through and pulled out a chair. Behind the muscleman came a young woman, who sat down in the corner with a notepad.

The latter was what caught Peter's attention, although his low blood sugar was making everything tough for him. He tried to greet the newly arrived goddess, but she brushed him off, so instead he extended his hand to the man with the blue eyes, who took it with a slight bow, but without introducing himself to any of us.

I decided to call him Pretty Putin.

"Well," said Ivan, "now you have seen the possibilities for cooperation."

Peter and I exchanged a puzzled glance.

"Do you mean the meeting rooms?" I asked.

He gestured as if he were a spokesmodel.

"Yes," Ingvill responded. "It looks great. What a wonderful place. I'd love to spend some time here."

"But what are we supposed to use the rooms for?" I asked. "The ones you showed us, I mean."

Everyone laughed long and hard at this question, but no one answered it. Instead Pretty Putin pulled out some small bags of chocolates and cookies and passed one to each of us.

"Present," he said.

"Thank you very much," I said as Peter ravaged his bag and inhaled his cookies.

"Good," he muttered to himself.

It was starting to get hot in the overcrowded room, and I could feel my armpits sweating. Besides, Pretty Putin was making me nervous, sitting there staring at us with those pale-blue eyes of his. I wondered what his academic specialty was and was about to ask him when Irina arrived.

"Hi," she said, nodding seriously and squeezing into the room.

"Hello," said Peter, standing up and creating a shower of cookie crumbs before elbowing me in the head in his eagerness to make it over to Irina and kiss her hand.

"You were enchanting last night," I heard him tell her.

"Thank you," she said, and turned to Ivan. "The dean is waiting."

Ivan leapt up and headed out the door with Ingvill, Peter, and me following. Pretty Putin, the woman taking notes, Irina, and a custodian-like guy who had just shown up presumably remained behind in the office.

We hurried past ferns, up the stairs, and squeezed through narrow hallways and past the old women who were still sitting idly on a bench. Ivan was moving so fast that Ingvill couldn't keep up, and I could hear her panting, trailing a few yards behind us up the stairs. When we rounded the last corner, I was sure we'd lost her, but whether she'd put a GPS tracker on Ivan or was equipped with an unusually good sense of direction, she managed to turn up almost in unison with us at the overcrowded antechamber to the dean's office, where the three secretaries were making a big show of our being way, way, way too late.

The dean's office was dark green with big, gleaming, heavily polished furniture. The dean welcomed us. He was just as big and well polished, wearing a blue suit and a light-green shirt that matched the walls impeccably. He had lips the same color as the rest of his face, eyelashes, and hair. He also had no neck and looked like he could have killed everyone in the room with his bare hands. Without saying a word, he gestured lazily that we could sit down at the meeting table, where the three secretaries

182

sat like stenographers, each with a notepad.

I sat down on the front edge of a chair and prepared to say something about how lovely the office was, but didn't have a chance to open my mouth before Ivan inhaled and then launched into a speech that lasted a good half hour. The whole time he talked he kept watching his own reflection on the table below him. Every once in a while he waved his hand in our direction, which I responded to each time with a smile and a nod.

Ivan's monotone mumbling settled like a membrane over the room. The shiny, polished desk reflected the sun and little motes of dust were suspended, motionless, in the light. The dean fell asleep after about ten minutes and ultimately his head lolled backward and he was snoring openly, while the three secretaries kept taking notes with such vigor that I almost suspected they were doing something else. Sleep tingled in my brain, and I glanced over at my two fellow travelers. Ingvill sat staring fixedly at Ivan, and Peter was slowly swaying back and forth looking like he was going into insulin shock.

Eventually Ivan finished talking and it got quiet. It was quiet longer than was strictly necessary, but apparently custom dictated that the dean should be permitted to sleep until he woke up on his own. In the end I couldn't take it anymore and tried warily to clear my throat a few times, which resulted in the dean slowly raising his head and staring us down with a look indicating that he had no idea who we were or why we were there.

I averted my gaze. I had the vague sense we had made some kind of misstep, a really big one. I thought about the chair. About the preschool-teacher program. About the unemployment office. About the KGB. About financial ruin. About how extremely lonely I would be in a basement apartment way outside of town.

And I smiled my broadest smile and opened my mouth right as a fourth secretary walked in, carrying three books that she placed on the table in front of us. The dean stood up and placed a business card on top of each of the books. The card said, "Vladimir Vesper. Dean of Faculty."

"Thank you," we said, making do with nodding to each person in the room since none of us had a business card ready to offer in return. "Thank you."

The dean walked over to a glass cabinet and took out a small picture that he brought over to the table and placed before us. It was an icon and seemed to be a depiction of Jesus holding his hands up in blessing. He was surrounded by a golden halo with the inscription ʻΟ ʼΩΝ in Greek.

I am that I am. God's words from the burning bush.

"What a beautiful icon," I said, but the dean brushed me aside.

"Friends," he said, gesturing toward the icon, "are to be treasured. Russia has never been to war with Norway. Norway has never been to war with Russia. Friendship."

He put his hand on his heart as he enunciated the last word and looked at us with his unreadable eyes, which didn't look the least bit sleepy anymore.

"Friendship," Ingvill repeated mechanically.

"Magnificent," mumbled Peter, picking up the icon from the table. "Absolutely magnificent. Reminds me of Rublev himself."

Only then did I realize that Ivan had stood up. He was standing by the door gesturing for us to join him. I leapt up and walked over to the dean, who kissed me on both cheeks and after that gave a giggling Ingvill the same treatment. Since we'd been talking about friendship so much, I decided to shake hands with all the secretaries as well. We were up to six of them now, and all of them smiled and nodded, especially pleased.

The last in line was Peter, who for his part was dragging his feet and hanging his head and looking quite sad, shuffling along with a limp plastic bag in his hand. Even his tweed suit looked sad, and I noticed there was a big brown stain on one lapel.

"Magnificent," he repeated mechanically as he took the dean's hand, "absolutely magnificent. Eternal friendship."

22

Back at the hotel I finally managed to get online, and the very first thing I accessed was an e-mail from the PTA president. "Dear Ingrid," she wrote, "please forward me the official municipal response on the right of children to have their shoes tied at school ASAP! Please also prepare a ten-minute summary for the next meeting. This will be one of the main items on the agenda."

I wondered if she actually thought this was one of the leading issues of the day, something our generation would be judged on after we were gone. The committee had always suffered from an inferiority complex compared to the legendary PTA that had stood on the barricades seven years ago to procure a new art room for the school. Everyone knew that feat couldn't be topped, but standing up for children's rights . . . maybe this was the closest you could get.

The next message was from the violin teacher, who wondered why neither Ebba nor Jenny had shown up for their lessons the last two weeks. "It makes our work that much more difficult when these little instrumentalists don't show up as agreed. Please review the home/school relationship bylaws (attached)."

Then there was one with "The Hobbit" in the subject line, but I scrolled right past that, moving on to an e-mail from Frank that had been sent to Ingvill, Peter, and me. "Call me," it said, "as soon as possible. We may have miscalculated our strategy."

This was followed by one from the chair: "Because of an unfortunate development related to the course revision, I've been forced to convene a departmental meeting that will also be attended by the ergonomics, occupational safety, and regulatory compliance officer, the dean of College of Arts and Sciences, and a representative from the university's Office of the General Counsel. Until that time, I would appreciate not receiving any anonymous letters in my mail slot."

I yanked on my hair and hit "Reply All" to Frank's e-mail: "Do NOT send anonymous letters to the chair! And I'm not part of any strategy!"

The response from Peter arrived promptly: "We're all part of the strategy, Ms. Bad Cop. ;-)"

I tried calling Bjørnar, but he didn't answer, so I sent a quick e-mail instead: "Things are OK here. Still alive. Glad Norway never went to war with Russia. How are you guys?"

Then I dialed the phone number for the Office of the City Clerk.

"Could I speak to whoever's responsible

for children's rights?" I asked the person who answered the main phone line and was transferred to the Office of School, Culture, and Leisure Affairs, which was apparently extremely busy, because I was on hold for a long time listening to panpipes.

While I waited, I picked up an English-Russian newspaper I'd found in the lobby. There was a picture on the front page of a sinkhole that had appeared in Siberia. No one knew why it happened. The article didn't make any attempt to explain it. No speculations.

I hung up the phone in the middle of one of Norway's top hits from 1989 and looked out the window where the snow was still blowing around. Maybe some of the flakes would end up in Siberia. Some might even stray down into the sinkhole that had opened without anyone knowing why. *Sinkhole.* The word made me think of something, some memory, without my being able to quite put my finger on it.

I Googled "sinkhole in Siberia." Articles from both American and British newspapers popped up. All of them agreed that the sinkhole was inexplicable, but they weren't afraid to speculate. Some thought the crater was caused by a UFO that had landed in Siberia and was now lying hidden at the bottom, but most were of the opinion that the collapse stemmed from Soviet-era test drilling in the seventies. Apparently they had been feverishly searching for gas in Siberia back then and had big plans to extract it, but eventually the project had been back-burnered when several big holes opened up on the surface of the earth. They were all lying there like open wounds in the landscape, and most of them were still burning because of the methane gas pouring out.

I pictured those burning holes. Like big torches or lighthouses, not showing the way to anywhere other than destruction and death. Just like the bonfires of those people who rob shipwrecks. Could you see them all the way from space? Maybe that's what had attracted the UFO here? Maybe that's why it came?

And if we were being invaded from outer space, how was I going to get home? Bjørnar had a lot of wonderful qualities, but he knew pretty much nothing about how to save a family from bloodthirsty aliens who had depleted their own planet and were now hoping for a piece of ours. My brain started tingling and the squeezing feeling was back in my chest. I closed my eyes and tried to think happy thoughts.

I went down to the lobby, where Peter was sitting in the bar with a glass of beer in front of him.

"Hi," I said. "Are you sitting here alone?"

"Actually, Ingvill's here, too. She's buying

herself a glass of white wine. She suggested we have a drink before we go to the Hermitage."

"The Hermitage?"

"Didn't you know about that? Ivan sent her a text message to invite us. I figured she would have told you?"

"Nope, she didn't."

"What didn't I do, Ms. Know-It-All?" asked Ms. Tropical Fruit Salad.

I rolled my eyes and walked over to the bar. It was completely silent in there with the exception of some quiet murmuring from a Russian news channel on TV.

"Bad news," Peter said when I returned.

"What?"

"A reliable source informs me that the dean won't approve the bilateral cooperation agreement between our respective universities," Ingvill said.

"Why? Things went so well at the meeting today. It was all friendship this and friendship that, in the past and the future and the present."

She scoffed.

"*You* thought it went well? Then you must not know much about Russian body language."

I wanted to tell her what I thought about her body language, but I refrained. Instead I turned to Peter.

"Don't you think it went well?"

"Yes, yes." He nodded, his mouth full of

cocktail nuts. "We got presents and everything. Nice presents."

Ingvill scoffed again.

"You guys are clearly novices when it comes to internationalization."

"That's true," I said, taking a sip of my wine. "And if I'm not mistaken, you've never been any farther east than the outlet mall just across the border into Sweden."

"Maybe we can make a better impression at tomorrow's meetings," Peter said, sounding hopeful. "Don't we have three of them?"

"Ivan said there's only going to be one. The other two were canceled. And of course it doesn't help that the icon disappeared. No, I think we're going to have to use the same tactic we're using back home. I can be the hard-liner, and—"

"What icon?" Peter interrupted.

"That picture the dean showed us. In his office," Ingvill said. "Ivan says it's extremely valuable. Priceless, apparently. If you ask me, it looked kind of junky. That Christ figure looked like something my niece might have painted. But anyway, it's gone. And apparently that's a problem for us."

"Why is that a problem for us?" I asked. "We didn't take it."

Peter looked down into his beer glass.

"Maybe not," said Ingvill, "but incidents like that aren't good for bilateralization. They lead to people looking for scapegoats. Studies have shown when that happens people tend to hammer down the nail that sticks out, so to speak. According to Ivan there's a heated search under way at the university right now. Apparently the dean is up in arms. And that's not good for anyone. I was supposed to meet Ivan tonight, but now he can't. Luckily we get to go to the Hermitage together now."

She stood up and walked over to the bar to buy another glass of wine. Peter gave me an odd look. He opened his mouth, but then closed it again.

"What is it?" I asked wearily.

"You know that icon . . ." Peter began.

"The Dean Icon?"

"Whoops."

"What do you mean 'whoops'?"

"I have it. In my room."

"What do you mean 'I have it in my room'?"

"What do you think I mean?"

"*You* have it? You mean you *took* it?"

I half expected him to start laughing and say the whole thing was some silly joke, but he just nodded gloomily and drained his beer glass.

"I thought it was a present!"

"A *present?*"

"I mean, they've been giving us gifts the whole time! Here, have some vodka. Here, have some chocolate. Here, have some mints. Here, have some of this and some of that. He was standing there talking about friendship and war and peace and, well, I was just absolutely sure he meant the icon as a gift. So I accepted it. On our behalf. On behalf of Norway. And a little bit for the Queen."

"You mean Queen Elizabeth?"

He nodded.

I tried to wrap my brain around what was actually an un-brain-wrappable situation. Blood pounded in my head, and the soles of my feet started to tingle. I pictured a flaming sinkhole. I took another large gulp of wine.

"*When* did you take it?"

"While you guys were hugging and kissing each other. I'd already stepped away from the table, but I went all the way back over and put it in my bag so we wouldn't come off as impolite. I mean, it's bad enough that we didn't bring any presents for them. Not bringing presents is a terrible move for internationalization."

"Not as terrible as stealing the dean's icon."

"It's not funny! Do you know what they're going to do to me? People get arrested for being gay here! I'm going to end up in one of those cages that punk band had to sit in. What was their name again?"

"Pussy Riot."

"Yes. And that finance guy . . ."

"Khodorkovsky."

"Yes, Khovsky! Pussy! In a cage! And then they'll send me to the gulag."

194

He glanced nervously in Ingvill's direction.

"Don't say anything to Ingvill," he whispered urgently.

"Why not? She's such a nice person, right? Plus, she's the hard-liner, not the bad cop, like me."

He gave me a resigned look.

"Ingvill *is* a nice person, but she's also a little too . . . into Ivan. She's sure to tell him. And then it's curtains for us."

"What do you mean 'us'?"

"We're in this together!"

"We are *not*—"

I was interrupted by Ingvill's return to the table with a fresh glass of wine. She looked even more dissatisfied now than when she first noticed I was in the bar. Actually her facial expression was kind of Glenn Close in *Fatal Attraction*, which scared me.

"What is it?"

"I just talked to Ivan. He can't go to the Hermitage with us. He's too busy at the university. Artemis is going to take us."

"Artemis is going to take us?" Peter repeated, looking a little happier. "Oh, I like him. He's a hoot."

"Who's Artemis?" I asked.

"I have to call Ivan back," Ingvill said, getting up. "He can't do this to us."

"No, don't bother. It's fine by me if Artemis

takes us," Peter tried to say, but she brushed him off.

"It's *not* fine," she said and stormed out of the room with her phone in her hand.

"Who's Artemis?"

"The one who grew up in Libya."

"Who?"

"The one whose father was a military adviser for Gaddafi. The one who had private lessons with Saif."

"Saif Gaddafi?"

"Correct."

"Have we even met this man?"

Peter chuckled.

"You can be quite funny. He stopped by a little while ago. I met him in the lobby. Had a lot of questions. Tons. He was particularly interested in you, actually."

"In *me?*"

Peter winked.

"But I don't even know who he is."

"You'll get to meet him soon."

"What kind of questions did he ask?"

"What kind of art we were interested in and what historical periods we liked, things like that. Clearly he's taking his job quite seriously. I think he really wants to help us get the most out of our visit to the Hermitage."

I pondered this information. I didn't like it.

"He's definitely a secret agent," I finally said.

"Who?"

"Artemis."

Peter chuckled.

"He's no agent."

"Hello? Libya? Military adviser? Gaddafi? Of course he's a secret agent!"

"He's definitely no agent! I served in the British Army and I certainly think I could spot an agent if I saw him. Or her. There are female agents, too, you know. Honey traps."

"No doubt he's coming to keep an eye on us," I said. "To find out if we have the icon. If it's as valuable as Ingvill says, anyway. No one really cares about these internationalization things."

"But internationalization is the reason we're here!"

"Yeah, yeah," I said. "Of course. But then you stole an icon and now we're in danger of being sent to the gulag or tossed into a burning sinkhole. And I can't sit in one of those little cages! I'm claustrophobic."

Peter sighed and we sat there, each staring into our own glass.

"What if we just take it back," I finally said. "Say it was a misunderstanding? Or a bad joke?"

"Take *what* back?"

"The icon."

"Oh, right. The icon."

I sighed as heavily as I could.

"Where is it now?"

"It's still in the gift bag with some chocolate."

"OK, I know what we'll do. We discuss the whole thing with Artemis when he comes to take us to the Hermitage. We tell him the truth— that you're not very bright, that you thought it was a present, and that the whole thing was a misunderstanding. Then everyone can stop searching for it. And we can have a good laugh."

"Yes," said Peter with a little start, "quite right."

But when I saw who Artemis was, I felt less confident about my own plan. Pretty Putin gave us a clipped bow.

"Are you ready?"

I gulped.

"Why isn't Ivan coming?" Ingvill whimpered.

"Ivan had an important meeting, unfortunately. So now I have the honor of escorting you."

He leaned forward and kissed Ingvill's hand, which made her look a tad more satisfied.

"Aren't you going to tell him now?" whispered Peter.

I pushed him away.

"Don't spit in my ear," I said. "I'll tell him when the time is right."

"Tell what?" asked Ingvill with a pout.

"Tell him about Norwegian wildlife," I said.

"Whatever," she said and walked unsteadily toward the front door with Pretty Putin, a.k.a.

Special Agent Artemis, while I swallowed the surprisingly large amount of saliva that had accumulated in my mouth. We were in trouble, big trouble.

23

Pretty Putin informed us that unfortunately he did not have a car at his disposal, and even though Saint Petersburg's subway system was supposed to be top-notch, he chose to place us in the icy wind next to a gray winter canal. By the time we finally reached the Hermitage, Peter's face was pale blue, and Ingvill's wine buzz seemed to have disappeared into a burning sinkhole.

We took off our coats and left them at the coat check, then waited for Pretty Putin to buy our tickets.

"What would you like to see?" he asked.

"Hmm," Ingvill said indecisively.

"I'd like to see the Italian Renaissance and Dutch Golden Age," Peter said. *"About suffering they were never wrong / the old Masters . . .* Isn't that how the poem goes?"

Our guide bowed briefly to Peter.

"The old Masters," Ingvill repeated, moving tentatively to stand beside Pretty Putin.

Then he looked to me, and I could feel his gaze trying to penetrate my skin and bones and all of me. Was this psychosomatic? I focused with all my might on blocking this out and wished I hadn't used up so much of my strength on panic attacks in the last few months.

"And you?" he asked. "What kind of art are you interested in seeing?"

"The Golden Age."

He nodded, sizing me up with his Putin eyes, and I swallowed again. In a panic. Because this *wasn't* psychosomatic. This was Voight-Kampff, the test they give replicants that measures contractions of the iris and invisible particles emitted by the body, to determine whether the suspect's response is empathic enough to tell if you're dealing with a human or not.

Someone informs you that your mother just died. How do you react?

You're at the Hermitage and are asked what kind of art you want to see. What do you say?

"Rembrandt and Brueghel," I whispered.

He got a triumphant look in his eye and I wondered what I had revealed. I didn't have time to think anymore about it, though, because now we were sweeping through the first floor at a whirlwind pace, up the ornate stairs and down three hallways, by niches and crannies, heading for the Golden Age.

I was grateful that Ingvill had laid claim to Pretty Putin. She was obviously a hundred thousand percent fascinated by everything he said, and he guided and gestured while she nodded, smiled, and giggled. At one point she even took his arm, but he wriggled free from her grasp by pointing at a painting.

Meanwhile Peter and I followed along behind, looking around at the paintings more or less at random.

"Why haven't you said anything about the icon yet?"

"Because I think he's giving us the Voight-Kampff test."

"The what test?"

"All you need to do is to act like you care about your fellow humans and say as little as possible."

"But I *do* care," he said, insulted.

"You didn't exactly give me the impression that you cared when I was the faculty coordinator, did you? Or when you forced me to be the bad cop? You *act* like you care, but you don't actually give a hoot!"

"That's—"

"Don't act like you have no idea what I'm talking about. We both know that you're mostly interested in covering your own ass."

He grinned.

"I could have helped you, you know."

"What do you mean?" I asked.

"I mean, you don't have to be the one who gets reassigned to the preschool-teacher education program."

I stared him in the eye.

"If not me, then who?"

He surreptitiously nodded his head toward

Ingvill, who was still trying to sneak her arm in under Pretty Putin's.

I closed my eyes and turned my face to the ceiling.

"Fine," I said. "If you guarantee that I won't be transferred, I'll do my best to clear up this icon business."

We shook hands.

"*Alea iacta est*," I said.

"*Omnes mundum facimus*," Peter said.

"What does that mean?"

"We all make the world."

We were standing in front of Rembrandt's *The Return of the Prodigal Son*, and I stared at it blankly. Looking at a father who believed he had lost his child forever. At a son, who finally found himself, in a space where he could raise his arms and stretch them into the air and feel free.

We all make the world.

My eyes filled with tears, until I could no longer see the son hugging his father tightly or the father receiving the son and saying that everything was OK.

Now you know who you are.

Now you have a center.

"I have to go to the bathroom," I told Peter.

He took me by the arm and said, "Remember what's at stake. You can't give in."

I hurried through the grand rooms and down hallways that were so cold the grandmothers guarding the art had to wear coats, shawls, hats, and gloves. I didn't pay much attention to my surroundings until I reached the bathroom and an intense ammonia smell hit my nose and eyes. Most of the other people in there had come prepared and were holding handkerchiefs over their noses and mouths, but I didn't have anything, so I threw up into my mouth several times before I was done.

Nor did I realize that the reason for the smell was that the toilet paper couldn't be thrown into the toilet, so I had to fish it out again using the toilet brush before depositing it in the open bin beside the toilet.

When I finally made it to the sink, there was no soap, but hopefully ice water would knock out the worst of the bacteria. My reflection made me think of the gulag again and how abysmal the toilet facilities there must be. I tried to distract myself with thoughts of unicorns and fields of wildflowers and had almost managed to pull it together by the time I found my group by da Vinci's *Benois Madonna*, where they were waiting in line behind a group of schoolchildren who were all trying to preserve the artwork for perpetuity on their cell phones.

"Weird how famous paintings like this are always so small," Ingvill said.

"You know so many things, Ingvill," I said, a statement that resulted in her mumbling something that sounded suspiciously like *slut*.

I tried to focus on Leonardo's interpretation of Mary's motherly love. She seemed so young. And I suppose she was, too.

When I had Ebba, I was twenty-nine. And with Jenny I was thirty-one. That was OK. But with Alva I was thirty-six, and I felt it right away: My body didn't want to be pregnant, and it definitely didn't want to give birth. The midwife said there was a kind of lip in there that hadn't gone away. The other two babies had just slid out without any problems, but Alva had built herself a wall so she could stay in the womb. For a second I felt like I'd made her homeless when I held her in my arms.

I longed for her little body, her rubbery rain-boot smell.

"Would you like to see the icon collection?" a voice suddenly whispered into my ear.

I closed my eyes and put up a mental wall before I remembered this was a Voight-Kampff test and that a wall wouldn't work. So I put on a smile and showed it to Pretty Putin in the hopes that it would dazzle him.

"The icon collection?" I repeated. "Definitely."

He stared at me and I sensed there was a battle burgeoning between us. The difference was that he'd trained in Gaddafi's Libya, whereas I pretty much only had what I'd learned from American movies. But maybe that would be enough?

"You're in a desert," I said, staring back at him. "You see a tortoise and flip it over so it's lying with its belly up. It can't flip itself back over without your help, but you do nothing. You just stand there and watch it suffer. Why?"

"Why?"

"Yes, why?"

"The tortoise must take responsibility for its own fate."

"But why did you flip it over to begin with? Why didn't you just let it be?"

He watched me without blinking.

"It needed to think things over a little," he replied, "reflect on its actions. No one is completely innocent."

24

That night I was constantly woken up by doors slamming shut and the heater cycling on and off, and every time I was pulled out of sleep, I felt the iron fist clench my heart a tiny bit harder. My throat responded by contracting as well, and my tongue was so dry it felt like it was made out of cardboard.

The bottles of water the hotel had set out as welcome gifts were already empty and no one answered the phone at the number labeled "Room Service," so I ended up drinking water from the sink in the bathroom, even though it was probably radioactive. At any rate it tasted strongly of chlorine, and I was dizzy and nauseated and wondered if I might have a fever.

In the end I got up, even though the night could hardly be described as over. It was snowing outside, but the ground was still bare. The canal was lit up a sickly yellow color and the streets were deserted.

I tried to go online, but received the same error message as before. Something about a PTC connection? That sounded strange, but everything was so strange in here, from the fluctuating heating system to the weird yellow carpet with its baroque-psychedelic pattern. Suddenly I felt the snow globe closing in to just this room.

Trapped in finite infinity.

And I would never find my way home. Not in time, not in space. Not on the inside, not on the outside.

If only I could get home, I thought. Then everything would work out.

If only I could find my authentic self, make myself a moveable home that could let me exist. That could pulverize the iron fist.

I turned on the shower. The water ran over me, and I closed my eyes and leaned my head back.

This wasn't one of those bathtub showers. This was a shower stall. A stall that was a portal that could start the process required to get me back.

To get me home from Russia. Home to us. Home to myself.

I'm not a replicant, I repeated.

I am a human being.

We all make the world.

It was all going to be OK.

I blow-dried my hair and slowly donned my socks and pants and sweater, then my coat, and peered cautiously out into the turquoise hallway. I slowly made my way down the stairs to the colorful lobby with its big black marble tiles and purple and yellow walls. There was an enormous sculpture in the middle of the room that at first I had thought was Atlas, until I realized that he wasn't carrying the world on his shoulders after all—he was trapped inside it. His body was muscular and sinewy, and it looked like he was pushing with his shoulders and his knees in an attempt to break out of the bonds that held him. This person was all about his intense need to escape, to free himself.

I tried to hold my thighs still, because they'd started trembling. I wondered if the best course of action might be to go back upstairs and open that bottle of vodka, now that I'd proven to myself that there was something outside my room. But the claustrophobia wouldn't let go and the trembling hadn't abated, either, so I pushed the bounds of my snow globe further still by putting on my hat and mittens and going outside.

There wasn't anybody in the street, though night was turning to day. The suburbs were probably jumping with people on their way to train stations or scraping ice off their cars. For all I knew, maybe Ivan was laboring right now to get his car into drivable shape while cursing internationalization generally and Norwegians specifically.

My thighs were still trembling, but now it was more from cold than anxiety.

I contemplated the icy wind from Siberia and my thoughts returned to that sinkhole. What would it be like to approach a crater like that? On foot over the Siberian tundra. An encompassing darkness that was suddenly penetrated by dancing flames and billowing gas that settled like a membrane over the land. I'd crawl toward the top of the tallest ridge and look down at the flaming opening.

What would I see?

What would I understand?

What would I remember?

Suddenly I noticed that it had stopped snowing and the canal lay covered in ice before me. I stared at the opposite shore, where the bluish buildings of the Hermitage stood out in the darkness. It had gotten to be six a.m. and traffic was already flowing in a steady stream.

Thoughts of the icon agitated me.

I pulled out my phone and called Bjørnar, who answered just as I was about to tap the red button with my finger.

"Good morning," I said. "You do exist!"

"Yes." He yawned. "Just barely."

"How's it going?"

"The way it usually goes when you're solo-parenting three kids and are busy at work."

"Yeah."

He yawned again and then asked, "How are you?"

"Fine. It's a little weird here. I wonder if I have a fever."

"Mm."

"Well, I just wanted to say hi. Make sure you weren't just a dream."

"Nope, I'm real."

"No news on the house?"

I regretted it as soon as I heard the words slip out of my mouth.

"The agent thinks we should consider taking it off the market."

"Oh?"

"So it comes up higher in the searches. There's no interest in it, not even from reptiles."

"Replicants."

"What?"

"You meant replicants."

"Anyway, nothing's happening. We're probably going to have to be prepared to own two houses."

"Don't say that!"

"I'm trying to be a little realistic."

"I know."

"We can talk about it when you get back. I have to hang up in a sec if I'm going to manage to get us all out of here on time. I have an early meeting."

"Say hi for me," I said flatly.

I looked at the canal and thought about gulags.

25

When I got back to the hotel, breakfast had just been served, and I sat down at a table conveniently positioned right behind a gigantic palm, but with a view of the lobby. Ivan turned up a few minutes later. He stood at the entrance to the breakfast room and looked around, but didn't see me.

I was nowhere. I was invisible.

Right up until I wasn't.

Pretty Putin bowed slightly, without saying anything.

"Hungry?" I held my plate up to him.

"I already had breakfast," he said.

"Lucky you. It's not that good."

He nodded uninterestedly.

"I don't know if the others are up yet," I said, "but Ivan was just here, if you're looking for him? He was wandering around in the lobby."

He looked tiredly up at the ceiling.

"I wanted to talk to you."

"To me?"

He nodded and pulled up a chair.

"What about?"

"About the purpose of your visit."

"Oh?"

I began to break out in a cold sweat. Truth

be told, I had no idea what the purpose was beyond general descriptions like *cooperation, internationalization,* and *synergistic potential.* After Ivan's crazy tour of the university, I had assumed that no one else had any idea, either, that everyone was just pretending.

I cursed the Voight-Kampff test.

I cleared my throat.

"The purpose of the visit is to negotiate the terms of a cooperative agreement."

"With whom?"

"Saint Petersburg State University."

"With what intentions?"

"Intentions?"

I took a sip of my coffee.

"Internationalization."

"Internationalization?"

I nodded.

"For students?"

"Bilateral ties at all levels."

"A broad exchange agreement then?"

"Innovation. Synergy. Professional lock-in. Mobility."

His eyes narrowed.

"I see."

"Do you?"

He nodded.

"I have to go now. Ivan and Irina will be here soon to pick you three up so that you can photograph the Neva. I understand that your colleague with the cowboy hat really wanted to see it."

"It's not a cowboy hat," I said. "It's an urban bowler."

"Why does he have it?"

"He's cold."

"But he bought it in America?"

"I doubt that. I bet he bought it in Hounslow."

"Where?"

"Hounslow."

"Can you spell that?"

He jotted down the name on a small notepad, bowed slightly, and disappeared into the lobby.

I counted slowly to sixty, then stormed out the same way and took the stairs three at a time up to Peter's room, where I pounded on the door until he opened it.

"Where did you put it?" I asked, forcing my way into his room.

"Put what?"

"The icon!"

"It's still in the bag."

I ran over to the table he pointed to and found the icon with a sad mix of half-melted chocolate.

"You can't store it like this! Look, you got chocolate on it."

I got a hand towel and started rubbing away the brown spots.

"I just talked to Pretty Putin."

"Who?"

"Artemis! He suspects us. I'm convinced. Oh, and we're going to go see the Neva with Ivan and Irina. They're definitely going to search our rooms while we're gone. We have to hide the icon somewhere they'll never find it."

"Go right ahead," Peter said and laughed hysterically.

"Why are you *laughing?*"

"I have faith in you. You've got this."

"I don't know," I said. "I don't like Artemis being so involved. If only we had duct tape!"

"I have duct tape."

"You do?"

"Of course. I never travel without it."

I considered asking what kind of travel he usually did but had no time to lose, so I started wrapping toilet paper around the icon and then stuck the little bundle into an empty pillowcase. I wrapped that in newspaper and used most of a roll of duct tape sealing it.

"Aren't you overdoing it a little now?"

"You can thank me when we're sitting on the plane home," I said, and thrust the icon and the duct tape under my jacket. "If anyone asks you, say you vaguely remember someone showing you a picture when we were in the dean's office, but you weren't really paying that much attention. You know nothing. Nothing! Got it?"

I swung the door shut on my way out and hurried down the hall as if I had a plan. In reality,

I had no idea what my next move should be.

I tried to think what a professional icon thief would do. Probably find an icon exhibit and slip this in with a bunch of cheap copies for sale. But I didn't have access to an exhibit like that, plus I'd already wrapped it all up.

Hiding it on our floor didn't make sense. They were sure to search there first. Maybe they were already setting up surveillance equipment.

But what about the top floor? I raced up the stairs and found myself in an exclusive bar with a view of large swaths of Saint Petersburg. There were big sofas and armchairs and little side tables featuring various types of orchids.

Not a customer in sight.

Not an employee in sight.

Was this wise? I couldn't think.

Plus I had to go to the bathroom.

I went right over to the farthest sofa, back in the corner, and used the rest of the duct tape to secure the wrapped icon to its underside. Without further reflection, I secured the mummified icon to the bottom of the sofa in the bar. Preserved it for posterity. Or antiquity.

Either way, it was hidden now. And could be forgotten.

If we just pretended like we'd never taken it, we'd start believing it ourselves. And then it would be almost impossible to figure out what was actually true.

Everyone knows that the replicants that are hardest to identify are the ones who don't know themselves. The ones who think they're humans.

"Chew on that, Voight-Kampff," I said to the empty room, to no one, and to everyone.

26

Most of the day was spent trudging along the Neva with Irina and Ivan. They didn't ask us any questions and hardly exchanged any words with any of us. At one point Peter asked if we could stop somewhere and eat lunch, but an icy look from Irina put an end to that idea. So we kept marching until she got a phone call and led us back to the hotel, where they deposited us with a small nod.

As I waited for the others in the lobby bar, I was actually able to connect to the Internet again. After I deleted the e-mails in my in-box from the PTA, the chair, and the alarm salesman (who had somehow mysteriously tracked down my e-mail address), I did a search for "stolen valuable art" and found a site called the Missing Art Database. "Icons" had their own category. Against my better judgment I clicked, but although there were several that looked like it, the Dean Icon Christ figure didn't appear to be in the system. On one side of the screen, there was a number you could call if you had information about any of the stolen artworks. It was the number for INTERPOL.

My body forgot how to breathe.

I could picture the headlines: "World-Famous Masterpiece Found in Hotel. Thieves Claim It Was a Gift." "Norwegian Government Unable to

Help Academics in Gulag." "Icon Ingrid Dead of Overdose." Because that was the worst thing. I was going to take the fall. Ingvill was completely unaware of what had happened, and Peter would wriggle his way out of the whole thing. Plus, he was a British citizen so the Queen would surely help him.

I, on the other hand, was in trouble.

"Where did you hide it?" Peter whispered when he came downstairs. His face was weirdly expressionless, and I wondered if the Neva stroll might have left him with permanent frostbite.

"It's best if you don't know."

"But I was the one who got it!"

"Stole it," I said. "Stole it."

"You *know*—"

I cut him off.

"We have to stop thinking about it, pretend it doesn't exist."

"Pretend what doesn't exist?" Ingvill asked.

"Nothing," I said.

"Nothing," Peter said.

"I wish *you* didn't exist," she said to me.

"And I wish you—" I began, but Peter elbowed me in the side.

"I think Irina's interested in you," Ingvill told Peter.

I started laughing uncontrollably, but stopped when I saw the look on his face.

"Why are you laughing?"

"I'm sorry, but she's not interested in you."

"How do you know that?" Ingvill asked.

"I know."

"*How* do you know?"

"First of all she looks like Nastassja Kinski."

"So?"

"And, by the way, Ivan is also completely uninterested in *you*."

Ingvill scoffed and walked over to the bar to buy herself a glass of wine.

"I'll have you know that she took my arm right before we reached the hotel," Peter said. "*And* said she was looking forward to seeing me again. Plus she wondered if we could meet, just the two of us. Tonight. Before the opera."

"What? When was this?"

"Right after she finished her phone call."

That silenced me for a second. And frightened me more.

"Peter, it's a honey trap!"

"What?"

"You mentioned them yourself, just yesterday! It's when a secret agent lures someone with access to sensitive information into an emotional relationship or, better yet, into compromising themselves, and then pressures him or her into spilling the beans."

"But Ingrid . . ."

"You said Irina wanted to meet you for a drink?"

"Yes, but . . ."

"It's a well-known fact that the Soviet intelligence system used a lot of honey traps. You know, back in the sixties, even the wife of Norway's prime minister got tricked."

"What?"

"Werna Gerhardsen, during a trip to Armenia. Apparently it's true."

"What?"

My head had started throbbing, and suddenly I was incredibly exhausted.

"Don't walk into a honey trap, Peter."

"Maybe I could just go a *little* ways into the honey trap, but without compromising any sensitive information? You know, kind of turn the tables? Besides, I don't know anything, anyway. You're the one with the icon after all. I've hardly even seen it."

The pounding in my head increased.

"Good news," Ingvill reported as she returned from the bar.

"Yes?" Peter said expectantly.

"What is it?" I asked warily.

"Ivan called. The Russian government extended our visas so we can stay two more days. We landed a meeting with the university president, which according to Ivan is like getting an audience with Putin. I shouldn't say so myself, but clearly there's a good chance that my transnational socializing skills have finally borne concrete results."

That was when it happened, right then, the terrible thing I'd been waiting for, the thing that had been lurking, lingering at the edge of my consciousness, the sinkhole that so far had been a sleeper cell, waiting to suck me in.

I had a vision of myself in the gulag. Bald, with a bunch of tattoos I'd given myself when I was high. How long would it take before I was addicted to opiates? Probably half a day. And then I'd have to turn tricks to get more heroin. Until I died of an overdose. Icon Ingrid.

I tried to call Bjørnar, but couldn't get through, so I had one of the amazons at the front desk call the chair of the department instead.

She was in an unusually good mood.

"I have to say, I had my doubts about you, Ingrid." She chuckled. "But this is looking really promising. Really promising."

"But I . . ."

"Go to the meeting with the university president and we'll let bygones be bygones. I'm going to meet with the administration here myself next week. As a department, we're not all that popular with them these days. A cooperative agreement with Saint Petersburg State University could turn everything around, in a jiffy. Do a good job, Ingrid, and all your mistakes—the defiance, the not coming to meetings, the mindfuckery—will be forgotten. I believe in you. Good luck!"

She hung up.

"But I have to go home!" I shouted into a black hole.

And I repeated that to Bjørnar once I had the same amazon dial him.

"I have to come home," I repeated. "We're moving."

"Well, there's home and then there's home," he said, deadpan.

"What does that mean?"

"Nothing. I'm just exhausted. We had to give someone a tour of the house this afternoon, and the place was a zoo. Alva was crying, and they just had to look around on their own because I needed to make dinner. And now I have to work all evening, because we have a contract that needs to be finished by Friday morning."

"I'm so sorry for being here and not there."

"We're going to have to postpone the move," he said, "until you come home. It's not like there's anyone who wants to move into this house right away, anyway."

"Postpone the move?"

My cold sweat was back.

"What did you think? That I was going to do it alone? We haven't even reserved a moving van yet. And we're nowhere near finished packing up the kitchen. And if you're going to be off dancing the kalinka for a few more days, I don't really see any other option."

"It's not that I *want* to stay here longer!"

He snorted.

"Obviously, but you have to. You said so yourself. To keep your job. And you need to keep your job. I mean, I earn plenty of money, but no one can make *that* much money. And besides, it's not like we're ever going to go to Russia on vacation, right?"

"Not even to visit me in the gulag?"

"If you end up in the gulag, you'll just have to do the best you can. I'll send you cigarettes so you can trade for deodorant and toothpaste, but we're not coming to visit."

"But surely the kids would want to see me?"

"I'll tell them you're dead."

"Dead?"

"Yup. Then I don't have to deal with all the fuss. Maybe we'll get a dog to replace you."

"But . . . To be or not to be?"

"Not if one of us is in the gulag."

He thought we were kidding around, and part of me was glad. Aside from the day I told him about this trip, it had been a long time since our communication had been anything other than a bare-bones exchange of information. But another part of me was dreadfully scared, and I broke into a cold sweat again, wanting to tell Bjørnar all about the icon and the misunderstanding and the possible secret agents and how the gulag thing wasn't actually hypothetical joking around.

How likely was it that this phone was bugged? In *Homeland* it took them only three or four hours to install cameras and microphones, and here they'd had a whole day. So the likelihood was probably around 170 percent.

"We're going to the opera tonight," I said breezily.

"What are you going to see?"

"I don't know."

"Well, have a good time."

"Thanks. Hope your day goes well. Sorry you have to man the ship alone. I know it's not easy."

"I'm just looking forward to it being over."

"Me, too."

I went up to my room and lay down on the bed, so that I was free to study the ceiling. The microphones were probably attached to the back of the pictures and the mirror. The cameras could be anywhere. The worst thing was that I couldn't find them and get rid of them, because that would make me look even guiltier.

I shut my eyes and breathed in and out and out and in, imagining life carrying on without me as I lay in a coma after an overdose.

After a car accident.

After an operation for stress cancer.

Right at this moment my body was so heavy and weary that I almost believed I had overdosed. If I hadn't been in the coma too long, Bjørnar would probably be sitting next to me holding my hand and saying things like, "Move your pinkie finger if you can hear me." But if I'd been unresponsive for a month or maybe even a year, there probably wouldn't be anyone sitting there.

By then I'd be alone except for the underpaid professional health care workers who came in once or twice a day to drain the urine out of me and wash me and massage my legs and talk to me about some singing contestant's most recent engagement or whether the skier Petter Northug was going to have to wear a house-arrest ankle monitor for his DUI. If it had been a really long time, Bjørnar would already have a new girlfriend and would be trying to decide if he should pull the plug on me or not. Or he would at least have gotten himself a dog.

I lay in bed and shivered and moved my pinkie finger and squeezed my hand into a fist. Just to be sure.

27

There was an annoying sound by my head.

I fiddled with my phone for a bit, but the noise didn't go away.

"Go away!" I cried at the room, but that didn't help, either.

It took a long time for me to realize I needed to answer the hotel's phone on the nightstand.

"Where are you?" a voice hissed. "We're late!"

"Deckard?" I mumbled, still half dreaming, my mind focused on replicant-related issues.

"Who? We're ready to leave for the opera. Everyone's here. You have to come down now, otherwise we won't make it."

"I'm in a coma. Go without me."

I hung up.

A little while later there was another infernal noise.

"Go away!" I cried again, but this time I had to get out of bed and shuffle over to the door to mute it.

It was Pretty Putin.

"I'm sick," I said. "I have to stay in bed. So if you want me to trudge along the Neva for hours on end, you can just forget it."

"You'll be healthy soon," he said and handed me a brown paper bag. "We're not going for a walk by the Neva. We're going to the opera."

"But I'm sick," I reiterated. "Fever, cough, maybe a sinus infection."

"Like I said, you'll be healthy soon. There's medicine in the bag."

"Aren't we supposed to meet the university president tomorrow? I'd better save my energy, sleep off the fever."

"Medicine in bag."

I tried to sigh, but it immediately turned into coughing.

"I'll be waiting in the lobby. You have thirteen minutes to get ready."

"Are Peter and Ingvill waiting in the lobby, too?"

"They went on ahead, with Irina and Ivan."

"Double honey trap."

He stared me in the eye, and it felt like he was searching for something. I tried to look as blank as possible.

"Fine," I finally mumbled. "I'll meet you in the lobby in thirteen minutes."

I walked into the bathroom and threw up. Then I opened the bag.

Tylenol, decongestant spray, and a bottle full of something that smelled strongly of alcohol. Pretty Putin had made his own diagnosis. Apparently good old-timey cough syrup was still available over the counter in Russia. I took two Tylenol, jammed the spray bottle into my nose, and took a few good swigs of the liquid in the little brown bottle, which immediately blazed a warm path down into my chest.

I took another swig, pulled a black wool dress over my head, tugged on one boot and then another, bundled myself up in my coat, and forced my body out the door and into the hallway.

On my way to the lobby, I took a detour past the exclusive bar on the top floor to make sure the icon was still there. That was a rookie move considering the entire hotel would be under surveillance by now, but I couldn't help it. I sat down on the sofa and discreetly felt around underneath until I found the bulky item.

For a second, it almost felt like the little package gave me an infusion of energy. And hope. It was as if it were radiating some kind of heat, and I started wondering if it really was a sacred painting. For all I knew, the dean might have gotten it from some functionary during his KGB days, in thanks for his assistance or as some form of bribe. In which case it really might be valuable. To a lot of people.

But right now it was mine and I rested my fingers on the warm, oddly comforting bulk for a bit before I took a deep breath and headed downstairs to fight yet another battle with Pretty Putin.

He blew off my suggestion that we take a cab to the opera, so I was forced to pull my hand-knitted wool cap down over my ears and stuff my hands deep into my pockets. My throat was scratchy and I wished I could find a place that sold lozenges. Saint Petersburg seemed to be full of scrap-metal dealers.

"You know it's a complete waste to take Ingvill to the opera," I said. "She's the world's least talented linguist."

He smiled.

"What are you smiling at?" I asked.

"Your alliance is already showing obvious cracks."

"There's no alliance," I said. "We've never been a team."

He didn't respond. He was probably trying to psych me out, but he'd forgotten to consider the cough syrup. Because although I was weak, it also felt like my insides were some kind of soft pudding or jelly, and I regarded my surroundings with a sense of indifference I couldn't remember ever having felt.

My entire youth had been filled with strategies—counting ten yellow houses, jumping over puddles, avoiding shadows, walking only on the left side of streets, thinking positively, anything to ensure my survival.

To ensure that things would go well.

Which they very rarely did. But I had Bjørnar. And the kids. And I was secretly confident that things would have gone much less well if I hadn't managed to count ten yellow houses or not worn my very best sweater. And even though these sorts of concrete strategies had evolved to become subtler and more focused on the power of my mind and the creation of magic shields, there was no doubt that my everyday existence was still filled with the whole same exhausting business.

I giggled.

"Why are you laughing?"

"I was thinking about Stalin. To be totally honest, he was a little funny looking."

He didn't respond.

"I guess it mostly comes down to how you feel about receding hairlines. Personally I prefer Gorbachev. Wasn't there a pop song about him? Do you remember the one I'm talking about?"

I started humming.

"How much cough syrup did you take?"

"The right amount."

The icon. That was what he wanted. We should have just given it back the first day. I could have brought it downstairs when we met to go to the Hermitage and said, "Look what I found on the floor," or "Look what Peter brought back from the dean's office. He thought it was a present. He's not all that bright." And then we could have bonded and become good friends. They probably already figured Peter had some kind of mental issue because of his urban bowler, so it wouldn't have been hard to convince them that he had been included in our group via some type of special program.

But for some reason I couldn't wrap my brain around at the moment, I had insisted that we hide the thing instead. And pretend we had no idea how or why it had disappeared.

And now I was going to die.

Not that it mattered. I mean, I'd been expecting that my whole life.

The catastrophe was finally here.

It was all over.

I thrust my arm into Pretty Putin's.

"We're best friends," I said. "BFF."

I could tell he thought I was becoming psychotic, and everything pointed to his being right. My mind reeled and I saw glowing spots on the street ahead of us. They were jumping around like little fairies. It was beautiful to watch.

"What are you talking about? You're like a—"

"A what?"

"A parrot! You talk and talk and make it impossible for other people to think. Can't you be quiet for two minutes?"

I hardly heard him. His voice was like the whistling wind.

"Quiet?"

"Be quiet? You? For two minutes?"

"Don't give in to hate," I said. "Order and chaos."

28

The others were still waiting in the lobby when we arrived at the opera house, so there was no way we were as late as Peter had made it sound. But I didn't have the strength to get into it with him. I made do with noting that they had, in fact, each walked right into their own honey trap. Peter was chuckling at something Irina had just said, while Ingvill was watching Ivan with rapturous eyes. He was looking down into a glass of wine.

"Ah, the Mariinsky Theatre," Peter said. "I've spent so many lovely evenings here."

"You've been to Saint Petersburg before?" I asked, surprised.

"Well . . . ," he began, but stopped and took a sip from his glass. "At any rate the opera we're going to see is wonderful. I'm sure I'm not far off if I say that this is the two hundred thirtieth time it's been performed?"

"That's right," Irina said with a nod. "Many people believe it is our foremost national epic."

"*Prince Igor*," I said, flipping through the program. "I can't recall ever having heard of it."

Ingvill laughed and tried to roll her eyes. It made her look like a constipated cow.

"Have *you* heard of it?" I asked, irritated.

233

"Of course."

"What's it about, then?"

"It's about Prince Igor, obviously."

"Prince Igor? Yes, and . . . ?"

She just smiled vacuously. She'd bought herself a glass of white wine. I thought about the cough syrup I had put in my purse and wondered if it would be a good idea to take another swig, but decided that it wasn't. Either way, it didn't taste good and it burned in my throat. Although the effect was good.

"*Prince Igor* is about men who go off to fight in a meaningless war, while the women stay home to do most of the work," Irina said.

I laughed and nodded my head knowingly, but Irina didn't seem to have intended any sarcasm. She gave me a scornful look and then took Peter by the arm and started pulling him down the hallway. She mumbled something about wanting to show him some interesting carvings.

That arm grab made me nervous, but there wasn't really any acceptable way for me to follow them. Besides, I wasn't feeling so good. I started flipping through the program to find out how long this epic was meant to last. Four hours, it said.

"I think I'll buy a glass of wine," I said.

"I'll join you," Pretty Putin said.

He led me up some stairs and into a narrow hallway, to a little bar where people were conversing quietly. I bought two glasses and handed one to him.

"Here."

"I don't drink."

"Are you sure?"

He took it, anyway, while I pulled out the cough syrup and poured a few drops into my glass.

"Do you think that's wise?" he asked.

"We can't always be wise," I said, giving it a stir with my finger. "Sometimes you just have to step on the gas to survive the turn."

"Why do you keep opening and closing your hand all the time?"

I looked down at my hand.

"Have you seen *Reversal of Fortune*?"

"No."

"It's about Sunny von Bülow, who was in a coma for twenty-eight years until she died in 2008. True story."

"And . . . ?"

"I'm kind of wondering if I'm in a coma right now."

"What makes you think that?"

"I don't know. Everything is so strange here."

"Typical Europeans. You make everything about yourselves."

"What do you mean?"

"You think all this"—he gestured around with his arm—"is something you made up? That it only exists in your imagination? What an ego!"

"I hadn't thought about it that way."

"Peter says you just bought a new house?"

"That's right."

"A very expensive house, if I'm not mistaken? You spent more than you'd planned?"

"Quite a bit more, yes."

"And you could use a little extra?"

My body went cold. He could tell, because a little smile appeared on his lips.

"May I give a little sage advice?" he said.

I nodded.

"Behave like a guest. Respect the host. Don't reach for more than your share."

The room started slowly spinning. I tried to find something disarming to say, but there wasn't anything.

Pretty Putin took a long drink from his wine-glass, placed it on a table, and moved closer. To the people around us we surely looked like lovers. Just like in that James Bond movie where he falls in love with a Russian agent. Who got shot and died.

"You know," he whispered into my ear, "that we have special prisons for women here in Russia."

"I see," I said shakily, trying to make it sound as if we were discussing everyday touristy sorts of things, but it was hard for my thoughts to keep up when he was standing so close to me. Besides, I suddenly felt really hot. I opened and closed my hand.

Fist.

Flat hand.

Fist.

Flat hand.

Pretty Putin took my hand and held it in a firm grasp.

It was like being anesthetized. Suddenly there were no words.

It was as if language didn't exist anymore.

He smiled and caressed my hair.

"If I were you," he said seriously, "I would consider very carefully what I was actually doing, what I wanted out of life."

I stared into those pale-blue eyes. A bell started to chime.

I wondered what he had actually said to me . . . if he'd said anything at all. Suddenly I was having trouble keeping track of everything.

"Honey trap," I mumbled. "Honey trap."

And before he could react, I raised my face a tiny bit farther and kissed him. His mouth was supple and tasted sweet.

I sucked on his lips. Sucked in all that sweetness, clarity, warmth.

Long enough that it was hard to separate again.

But in the end he took hold of both my arms and pushed me away.

"That," he said, "wasn't OK."

"Sorry," I said. "But you—"

A new bell started chiming for me right then, and Pretty Putin pulled me back down the hallway and into the auditorium, where Prince Igor was preparing to take back what was his.

29

It was not entirely clear to me whether it was due to the fever, the cough syrup, or my lack of familiarity with the culture, but the plot of the opera seemed completely incomprehensible. Thanks to the subtitles rolling across the screen at the bottom of the stage, I was able to tell that vodka played a big part as well as defiling women, and when it came to Prince Igor himself, I got that hubris was a major issue with him.

Because, like so many tragic heroes before him, Igor was totally out of step with his surroundings. Even though a solar eclipse took place right as he declared war against the Cumans, and even though the sobbing princess, Yaroslavna, pleaded with him to reconsider his plans and stay home, he pushed right on through with his plan. Naturally this resulted in his being taken captive immediately, which in turn led to famine and hardship throughout all of Russia.

That pretty much seemed to be the gist of it, but there were quite a few minor characters that I didn't get the point of, not to mention that they all had names that made them sound like bad guys, like Ovlur, Skula, and Yeroshka. I felt dizzy and weird, and at one point I might have fallen asleep with my head on Pretty Putin's shoulder.

During the intermission the others went to buy more wine, but I couldn't face getting up. I was certain I had a fever. It was eating its way through my body, and the tickle in my throat kept compelling me to cough. I took another swig from the brown bottle and observed that no one had asked how I was doing or if I wanted to take a cab back to the hotel.

It was like that summer when I had pneumonia.

The nights were so long.

I lay there as quietly as I could, waiting for the rest of the family to wake up.

Five.

Six.

Seven.

Seven thirty.

I could hear them moving around—the click of the coffee machine, the radio turning on, buttering their toast, reading the paper, mumbling to each other.

I wanted to call out to them. Yell that I missed them. That I didn't have the strength to lie there all by myself. That I was scared. But it hurt to breathe. Talking was out of the question.

My memories of those weeks involved my mother poking her head in the bedroom doorway when they were ready to go.

"We're leaving now," she reported.

Thumbs-up.

"Hope you feel better soon."

Nod.

When they came home, it was the same procedure. They set things on the kitchen counter, turned on the radio, got out pots and pans, set the table.

I couldn't understand it.

Why didn't they come check on me, say hello?

I recovered after a week, but the loneliness wouldn't release its hold on me.

It had never released its hold.

The pneumonia didn't cause it. It just put words to it.

I was alone.

"I have to go back to the hotel," I said when Pretty Putin sat back down next to me.

"You have to see the last act," he said firmly. "There's only an hour and a half left."

I moaned and tried to find a comfortable position, but all the stuff going on onstage kept bothering me. The last act was really a hot mess. The only unifying motif seemed to be an overfondness for bird metaphors. As far as I could tell, Khan Knichak was like a raven, who swooped down and brought the Russians grief. Igor for his part was more like a falcon. These allusions bordered on being understandable. No one likes ravens. They're unreliable trouble-makers devoid of self-discipline and integrity. Can't do anything on their own, just scrounge off others.

Not like a falcon. A falcon is a leader.

You can't capture a falcon.

I could picture it as I sat there. So high up that it couldn't even hear the falconer.

The widening gyre turning.

Things falling apart. The center that cannot hold.

And mere anarchy is loosed upon the world.

The bells rang.

The Cumans were approaching Putyvl.

But Igor came running on the stage and flung himself into the battle against the Cuman hordes with his sword in hand while Yaroslavna clutched at her heart.

After that I don't remember anything.

I tried to find the hotel, but when I knocked on the doors at each building, a dog opened and explained that no one was home. And the landscape was so odd, so unrecognizable. Maybe it was just me, but I couldn't find my way.

30

There was no way to know what time it was, but outside the window it appeared to be night, because the streets and the canal were shrouded in darkness. A lady in a babushka slowly made her way down the street before disappearing around a corner.

And then there was no one.

My head throbbed dully, and the veins in my temples were swelling. My sinuses ached.

I squirted my nose and pulled out the brown bottle, which somehow was almost empty. The label didn't indicate how much you should take in a day. I couldn't even find the little pictogram Norwegian medicine bottles have to warn you not to drive while taking it. I took a little sip, and then one more.

I thought about the icon.

Maybe it would be wise to check if it was still there. If someone had followed me earlier in the evening, they might have removed it from its hiding place. Was it still up there radiating light and hope?

I pushed myself off the bed, forced my feet to climb up two flights of stairs, ordered a glass of Georgian wine, and sat down on the corner sofa. There was hardly anyone there. Two men in silk shirts focused intently on their conversation at a window table, and a woman sat at the bar looking bored. I wondered if she might be a prostitute. In movies prostitutes always sat at the bar and waited for men to pick them up.

I regretted not having brought a book with me. Now people would probably assume *I* was a prostitute. But then I remembered that I wasn't wearing any makeup and hadn't brushed my hair or changed my clothes. Plus I was sick. All things considered I should be pretty safe.

The cough syrup was still working well, and the little fairies had come back, too. I reached out my hand to touch them, but they eluded me every time. They were too fast, way too fast.

As fast as Pretty Putin, who was suddenly sitting in the chair in front of me with a glass of whiskey in his hand. I stretched my hand out again to see if he was real. He was.

I giggled, while at the same time carefully creating a magic shield between him and the duct-taped icon.

"I thought we put you to bed?" he said tiredly.

"But now I'm awake."

He rubbed his eyes.

"Did you take that whole bottle of cough syrup?"

"Maybe, maybe not."

He opened his mouth, but was interrupted by Peter, who entered the room huffing and puffing.

He didn't seem to see me, because he ran straight over to Pretty Putin.

"There you are," he said. "I can't find Irina anywhere! Where could she be?"

"I don't know."

"She said to meet her in the bar by the lobby."

"It'll be fine," Pretty Putin said. "Your colleague is sick."

"Ingvill is sick?"

Pretty Putin nodded at me.

"You!" Peter said, as if he'd forgotten I existed. "I thought we put you to bed?"

"I'm fine," I said. "I slept a little. And then I took some medicine. Oh, and here's a glass of wine. So, I'm doing fine. No need for concern."

I raised my glass in a kind of cheers, which made Peter raise his eyebrows.

"Why are you raising your eyebrows?"

"No reason."

"Should *I* raise my eyebrows at how you're running around chasing all the women you can find here in Russia? At how you're acting like we're not on the same team, even though you've always *said* we are?"

"Did you know that—"

"Maybe you should go look for Irina," Pretty Putin interjected, "if she said she would meet you? She's usually quite punctual."

"Of course," Peter said with a little bow. "Of course."

And before I could say another word, he was out the door.

"He's an idiot," I said.

Pretty Putin didn't say anything. I didn't even know if he'd heard me. He glanced out the window at the snow, which was doing its usual blowing thing. He looked like he was far away. I wondered how far away he was. If he was all the way out at that sinkhole.

"You're coming on too strong," he finally said. "Russian women are subtle. They know what men like."

"What do men like?"

"A certain mystique, coyness. Men like to take the lead. There needs to be a sort of dynamic in the relationship—one who gives and one who receives. Otherwise it's like a head-on collision."

"But I'm not trying to hit on Peter. Sure, he does have a Bill Nighy–esque quality, but I'm not interested in him. Absolutely not. And besides, he *is* an idiot. It's only right that someone tell him that."

"You're coming on too strong," he repeated. "There's nothing left. Everything's been said. It's like I said before. You're like a parrot."

"Well, this parrot has to go to the bathroom," I said.

The little fairies parted politely as I got up. I was still a little hesitant for fear that the invisible shield between Pretty Putin and the icon would disappear with me when I went. But they must have kept it going for me, because when I glanced back, he wasn't showing any interest at all in the sofa. He was staring blankly out at the snow again. He looked lonely. I longed for Bjørnar so much my chest ached.

Luckily some cough syrup helped.

Although now there was less than a quarter of the bottle left, and a small wave of panic started to build in me.

I decided to ask Pretty Putin to get me some more. Maybe I could even use the icon as a bargaining chip to get more bottles? Enough to bring home so that I could hold on to this numbness forever. And never have to give up the little fairies. They could hover over the road ahead of me, no matter which way I decided to go.

I giggled at the thought and walked out into the hallway on unsteady legs.

Just then Peter came walking toward me.

"Hi," I said smoothly. "What's up?"

"She threatened to kill me!"

Only now did I notice how pale and haggard he looked.

"Who?"

"Irina. She said that if I don't bring the icon back within twenty-four hours, she's going to shove my testicles so far up my body they would come out my nose."

He put his hand up to his nose, looking like he could imagine how just such a maneuver would feel.

There was a faint whooshing in my head, while at the same time I was having trouble processing what he had said. But I couldn't deny that the idea of shoving Peter's testicles out his nose had occurred to me as well, several times.

"You're an idiot," I said.

He stared at me without answering.

"We have to return the icon," he said.

Images of myself on the floor of a small cell flickered through my head. Drugged and brain dead. Lobotomized and ugly. And what about Peter? He wouldn't last one week in the gulag.

I started to cry.

And then Peter started to cry.

"What's with you guys?" called Ingvill, who walked up right then.

"We're just a little sad," I said. "And scared."

"Why?"

"Peter's concerned about internationalization. That things won't work out with the . . . bilateralization."

"How drunk *are* you?"

"Not drunk enough, Tropical Fruit Salad, not drunk enough."

"I'm meeting Ivan in the bar," she told Peter. "Are you coming?"

"Peter's tired," I said. "He wants to go to bed."

"Really? I would have thought maybe *you* were the one who ought to go to bed. You're a true embarrassment to our country. An embarrassment! Getting drunk like this."

"At least I'm not roaming around massaging people," I muttered.

"As if you haven't been busy engaging in activities like that with your students? Oh, please."

"What are you talking about? I have most assuredly never done anything like that."

"I know what mindfucking is, let's just say that."

"She doesn't think that mindfucking is sex, right?" I asked Peter. "Please tell me she doesn't think that."

"You think you're so much better than everybody else," Ingvill said.

"All right, ladies," Peter said, holding his hands up to try to defuse the situation. "We're all going to go get a beer together now. For the sake of internationalization. What do you say?"

I sighed.

As did Pretty Putin.

We sat around the table in the bar at the top of Designa Hotel in Saint Petersburg without saying a single word. Around us the snow swirled in its usual manner, around and around, probably not landing until it reached the Himalayas. Or some other high-altitude place. Some mountain where at this very moment a Mongolian Prince Igor was releasing a falcon to soar up, up, up into the big wide sky. Until it was just a black dot, hardly visible to the human eye.

Things were clearly falling apart.

Someone elbowed me.

"What?"

"Artemis wonders if we know anything about the icon? That one that disappeared from the dean's office."

"A dingo took it."

"What are you talking about?"

"Maybe a dingo took your baby!"

I cracked up, loudly, wondering if they even got the reference. I couldn't remember where the line came from, but it was somewhere funny. Bjørnar would know.

"All you have to do is knock your heels together three times and command the shoes to carry you wherever you wish to go."

I lay back on the sofa, closed my eyes, and felt someone pick me up. I put my arms around Pretty Putin's neck. Now I would tell him everything. Calmly and honestly, I would explain that Peter had made a stupid mistake because he was a stupid man, and that the icon was taped to the bottom of the sofa he'd just picked me up off of, and all he had to do was unstick it and take it with him.

Then everyone could be on the same team again. I opened my mouth.

"Take me to your leader," I said with a giggle.

"Shut up now," he said calmly.

So I did. And I let myself be carried to a bed, where wondrously gentle hands tucked me in and tenderly caressed my cheek. It was so delightful and soothing. Human warmth. Someone who cared. And I tried to stretch toward the warmth, until the whole scene was pierced by a sharp voice.

"Did you get it?"

It sounded like Irina. I tried to raise my hand in a polite greeting, but my arm wouldn't move, so I sent a signal with my eyelids instead.

"*Nyet.*"

They switched to speaking Russian. Diphthongs and consonants with variations that drew me into a darkness that was suspiciously reminiscent of Tehom. The deep that even God seemed to fear. That the Spirit of God made do with hovering over. That was only released one single time in history, in the days when God let the Flood flow over the earth.

I sank. Sank.

Until I was swirling with the other snowflakes.

Further and further. Without our ever having thought of falling.

My only thought was to stay afloat until I made it home to Bjørnar, and he could receive me.

When I woke up again, I was scared and called home.

"You woke me up."

"If someone asked me who you thought was the best-looking man in the world, I would say that soccer player, Lars Bohinen, or David Byrne. Is that right?"

"Huh?"

"You said one time that you thought Lars Bohinen was good looking. But I think maybe you think David Byrne is better looking. Is that right?"

"Ingrid, I—"

"Right, we'll cross off David Byrne."

"What's your point here?"

"To be or not to be isn't enough. Under normal circumstances it would be enough, more than enough. But something happened to the universe. It's off-kilter or something. The gyre is widening. Or there's a sinkhole. I don't know. We have to take precautions. Come up with some lists."

"Ingrid, stop. Just listen—"

"And not just for this dimension. We need to think about the next world, too. After we're dead. You have to promise you'll find me. Do you promise?"

"You need to be quiet now and listen to me. First of all, are you drunk? I hope you're drunk, because if you're not, you're psychotic. Are you drunk?"

"I have a sinus infection. And I took a weird cough syrup. And I don't want to be here anymore. I want to come home to you and the kids. And I don't want to be scared anymore."

I started sobbing into my cell phone.

"OK. You're going to go to bed now and sleep. And you're not going to call me again until you're sober. We have a history of people from your side of the family calling other people when they're drunk and then regretting it later. You know this."

"Yeah, but we have to be able to answer—"

"Call me back when you're sober. Go to sleep now."

"OK. Sorry."

"Stuff your apologies in a sack and go to bed. Enough."

31

When I woke up the next morning, my first impulse was to take more cough syrup. But I felt cold and clammy and had a disgusting metallic taste in my mouth, as if I'd been sucking on a handful of loose change all night.

Enough, I repeated to myself as we found ourselves in a busy hallway outside what I assumed was the university president's office. People hurried past in all directions, with books and papers and bags and umbrellas. We sat completely still. Peter's face was ashen and Ingvill was checking her e-mail on her phone. I felt dead inside.

Sorry, I texted Bjørnar. *Sorry about everything.*

The preschool teacher contacted me, he texted back. *She said you've been acting weird at drop-off and pickup, and that one time you smelled like alcohol. We have to discuss this when you come home.*

I put my phone back in my pocket.

"What did you guys tell them yesterday?" I asked Peter and Ingvill, noting that it hurt to speak.

"Who?" Peter asked.

"Who do you think?"

"All you said was *them*. That could be anyone!"

254

"You are such an idiot," I said. "I mean Pretty Put—Artemis and Irina! And Ivan."

"Nothing. *You* told me I shouldn't say anything!"

Ingvill's cow face slowly looked up from her phone.

"What wasn't Peter supposed to say anything about?"

"Nothing."

"Ingrid," Peter said, "I think we should tell her."

I put my face in my hands and rubbed my forehead as hard as I could.

"Fine," I said. "He wasn't supposed to say anything about how he took the icon because he thought it was a present and how I hid it."

Ingvill got that expression on her face that suggested there wasn't much going on in her head.

"Icon," she repeated slowly.

"The dean's icon."

"What do you mean?"

"The icon that disappeared from the dean's office that everyone's been looking for. We have it."

"Why do we have it?"

"Because we were scared to give it back. We were scared it would ruin our chances of reaching an agreement."

"What agreement?"

"With the Russians."

"With Ivan?"

"Yes, Ingvill, with Ivan. We're all pinning our hopes on him. He's Mr. Internationalization."

I rolled my eyes.

"Oh! You *know* you're not allowed to roll your eyes at me!" Ingvill exclaimed. "I'm making a note of that right now, and I'm going to report you to the chair when we get home. And then we'll see!"

"Maybe you could add that I mindfucked you by using difficult words that you didn't understand—like *internationalization*."

"This is no joking matter, Ingrid," Peter said. "Who knows what they're going to do to us now? I did say you should return it. And this whole time I've been trying to convince—"

I slapped him in the face.

"Now you listen up, you British eel! All I've done is protect you! I didn't even need to *touch* that stupid icon. But I helped you, and hid it for you. I was on your team. And this is the thanks I get?"

I stood up, raised my hands in the air, and yelled, "PEOPLE SUCK!"

A hush came over the busy hallway. People turned to see where the outburst had come from, the outburst that had echoed from the outermost corners made of plaster slathered with layers of asbestos-ridden paint, the outburst that appeared to have come from an almost forty-year-old woman wearing her best black outfit with her hair up and mascara and lipstick. Why was she wearing that? Not because she wanted to look pretty, because she needed a suit of armor.

Because I was scared. Scared of the past, of the future, of the other people, that love would end, that I would be alone, that death was something dreadful, and that I would never, ever, ever have a home.

That this was the end. My own true, final, and completely personalized apocalypse, which I'd been waiting for all along.

But they couldn't see any of this.

Partially because of the suit of armor, which guaranteed me a semblance of normality.

Partially because right at this moment, in this brief instant in the infinitely long time span of the universe, I didn't feel scared, but angry.

Which in turn scared me even more since I remembered the end of *Star Wars Episode VI* and knew that anger is a step toward the dark side, which made me even angrier. Because I was also tired of movies scaring me. Tired of worrying that someday I would wake up in a Matrix pod. Tired of remaining vigilant, on the lookout for men who might be walking around wanting to make a woman suit out of my skin. Tired of being afraid of suddenly realizing that for years I'd been repressing the murder of my family.

Tired of being afraid of feeling all right in the event that *not* feeling so all right might be what created the magical shield that would protect me from things *really* going downhill, in which case doing fine would sadly open me up to all kinds of horrible and awful occurrences and experiences that the universe could decide to fling at me.

"MOTHERFUCKING ASSHOLES!" I screamed so loudly it felt like my jaw might snap.

And that included the movies, books, comics, the universe, Tehom, and myself.

I was sick of it!

So terribly and infinitely sick of it all.

Someone took me by the arm.

"LET GO OF ME!" I yelled, turning around.

"Be quiet," Pretty Putin said through his teeth.

"You be quiet."

He slapped me. Not hard, but enough to sting, and the shock of it brought tears to my eyes. I tried to hit him back, but he grabbed my arm.

"You have to be faster than that if you're going to hit anyone other than the cowboy there," he said with a nod in Peter's direction.

"It's *not* a cowboy hat, I told—"

As usual Pretty Putin waved the words away with a hand gesture.

"The president is ready now."

We slowly rose and marched in, Ingvill first, then Peter, then me, and finally Pretty Putin and Irina.

As we crossed the threshold, I gasped.

This whole time I had envisioned the meeting taking place in the president's office.

But what we were looking into now was very clearly a courtroom.

Row after row of benches. Two long tables next to each other. A raised desk at the front, with two witness boxes on either side and along the wall to the right. Incontrovertible.

Indisputable.

A cage.

A trap.

And I realized that if I walked into it, I would never come out again.

So I took an automatic step back, which resulted in my walking smack into Pretty Putin.

I turned around to face him.

"I have to go to the bathroom."

He gestured with his hand that I should move farther into the room.

"Peter did it," I said. "It was him the whole time."

Irina took my arm and shoved me into the room.

"I don't want to," I said.

"*I* don't want to go to Omsk," she said, nudging me in farther. She kept going until they signaled us to take a seat at the oval table at the very front.

"I'm not going into the cage," I said.

She laughed briefly and sat down on the bench

259

behind the table, along with Pretty Putin and Ivan.

Ingvill, Peter, and I sat down at the long table in silence. And waited. Well, Ingvill typed something into her phone. It seemed like she'd had Internet access most of the time. Either that or she was playing Candy Crush.

A few moments later a strange procession of people turned up. First a whole bevy of secretaries, carrying stacks of paper and folders and writing implements. After that came the dean and five other men I thought I'd seen on Ivan's tour, but whom I couldn't quite place. I was very sure that one of them was the custodian, who seemed to keep turning up in the university's numerous rooms and lecture halls the day we'd taken our tour. Although today for some unknown reason he was wearing a suit. Stalin style. Maybe this was actually his day off, but he'd been called in for jury duty?

My head was pounding. I thought about the cough syrup, which was sitting on my nightstand. I thought about Sunny von Bülow. If your name was Sunny von Bülow and you could strut around wearing Chanel, an opiate addiction wasn't so bad, but for the rest of the world's population it was just ugly and pathetic. I shouldn't have taken so much, and I certainly shouldn't have called Bjørnar.

Suddenly I thought about the cough-syrup lady

from the open house. What if she had actually been a future version of myself, who had been sent back in time to warn me of my boozy, drug-dependent future? Sent back to the very beginning, to the moment when I made the wrong choice.

I tried to tell myself that I was standing in a golden forest and ahead of me there were two paths. Two paths that diverged. Sometimes there was a right path and a wrong path, one that was overgrown and narrow and one that was wide open, but from where I stood, it was hard to see which one led where.

The question was only if I'd already made my choice.

If the path was buying the house.

If the path was the cough syrup.

If the path was the art heist.

If I was still standing in the forest, contemplating the paths.

The pounding in my head and the cold, clammy feeling increased and were amplified by the custodian, who had taken a seat in the judge's chair and was now slapping the table in front of him repeatedly with the palm of his hand. Weirdly enough it seemed like the people up front were goofing around, because they were all smiling and laughing, and the four other men joined in on the playful banter as well. They seemed like they were about to whip out a tray of smoked trout and vodka and have a party.

261

But the gaiety did not extend to Ivan, Irina, or Pretty Putin. When I turned around, I saw that they were all sitting stone-faced, staring straight ahead.

This was very clearly psychological warfare. And when was the university president actually going to arrive?

Suddenly I understood the game plan. Of course! He wasn't coming. The only one coming was the so-called janitor who was clearly KGB and whom Pretty Putin, Ivan, and Irina had no doubt been reporting our movements to for ages. And now he would sit as judge in this ridiculous courtroom, which was probably used as a law-school lecture hall, but which *could* also be used for real if someone played punk-rock music in a church or stole a priceless artifact or something.

I closed my eyes, put my head in my hands, and prepared to have a panic attack of epic proportions. But it didn't happen. The seconds ticked by, but to my surprise I wasn't predominantly scared. Actually, I was still angry. More importantly, I felt no need to contemplate this any further or gauge whether it was some kind of side effect of the cough syrup that had caused me to walk around giggling and seeing fairies. Instead I had the overwhelming sense of having had enough.

And the next instant, I was standing up and

slapping the table as hard as I could with my hand. So hard, actually, that I was worried I might have broken something. But the anger deadened the pain.

"Enough!" I shouted. "*Enough* already! I can't take any more! Are we bad guests who didn't bring hostess gifts? Yes. Are we clueless about what you consider the fundamental ground rules of politeness? Yes. Was this committee put together without any consideration for whether its members actually knew anything about internationalization mechanisms or bilateral cooperative agreements between public universities? Yes. Are we here primarily because we're scared of being reassigned to the preschool-teacher education program and/or because we're trying to get each other reassigned? Yes. Did we somehow misinterpret the gesture of being shown a valuable icon? YES!"

No one had interrupted me yet, so I took a breath and continued.

"But we're all human beings. Look at us!" I flung my arms out to the sides in a dramatic gesture meant to also include the custodian and all his secretaries. "What is the question that we must all ask ourselves? The question is . . ."

I paused, trying to think up a good question.

"Is it worth it? Or, to put it another way, should we be—or not be? Am I right? For what is it that makes us bear those evils we have, instead of flying to others that we know not of? The heartache and the thousand natural shocks. That we *all* endure."

As I enunciated the final sentence, I made another sweeping gesture to include the custodian and everyone else in the room, but the former merely watched me calmly with his dark eyes, his expression unchanging.

Still, there was no turning back now. So I kept going.

"*Omnes mundum facimus*," I said slowly. "We all make the world. For there are ravens out there. They swoop down and ravage the land. But we aren't ravens! We're falcons! And when the falcon cannot hear the falconer, we're all in big trouble. That's when the indignant desert birds swoop down. That's when darkness falls. But we are falcons and we will not let darkness fall. We all make the world."

There was silence. For a long time.

For just as long as I'd spoken. And that was a long time, for a speech that didn't consist of a single point beyond a few fragments ripped from Hamlet's soliloquy, Yeats's "The Second Coming," and what I remembered from *Prince Igor*.

In the end the custodian walked over to the secretary who had been simultaneously interpreting my speech and mumbled something into her ear.

"Would you like to say anything else?" she

asked me as she continued to jot down everything that was said in her notepad.

"Just that Norway and Russia have never been at war," I said. "And you can't say that about very many countries. We're a team. In a way."

I put my hand on my heart the same way the dean had done a few days earlier.

"Friendship," I said loudly.

She translated yet again for the KGB custodian, who rolled his eyes and said three brief words in return.

Silence again.

"Isn't she going to translate?" Peter whispered to me.

I wanted to say that she didn't need to.

Because it was obvious what he'd said.

I glanced over at the cage and gulped.

So this was how it ended. No dignity and no hope. I should have known.

I bowed my head and prepared for the sword blow.

But then the silence was broken by applause. And the next moment the custodian was next to the whole useless Norwegian delegation, hugging and kissing Ingvill, Peter, and me, as he let out a long stream of words that the secretary struggled to interpret quickly enough.

She abridged it to, "He says that you have an agreement."

"An agreement?" I asked, confused.

"A cooperation agreement," she said with a stiff smile. "Congratulations. This has never happened before."

"But who do we have a cooperation agreement *with?*"

She looked at me as if I were an idiot.

"University President Akady Morgarich approves the cooperative agreement between your university and Saint Petersburg State University. For *the very first time* we will enter a bilateral agreement with a Western university. This is a historic day. A day for friendship. And for happiness."

"The custodian is also the university president?"

"Shut up," Pretty Putin whispered into my ear.

"I'm shutting up now," I said. "Do I need to sign something?"

"I'll take care of that," Peter said. "I mean, you've been sick. Go on back to the hotel, Ingrid. I'll handle the rest of this."

He gently pushed me away and I was too exhausted to protest.

I just said, "Fine," and walked out into the hallway. Away from the courtroom, away from the custodian who was also the university president, and away from my two so-called teammates.

I stood there out in the hallway, feeling the adrenaline run out of my body and evaporate, to be replaced by . . . nothing.

Not anxiety. Not emptiness. Not numbness. Not depression.

Just nothing.

"I'll drive you back to the hotel," offered Pretty Putin, who was suddenly standing beside me. "Today I have a car."

"All right," I said.

32

I expected him to just drop me off, but instead he parked the car and came inside with me. Without a word, I headed for the stairs, walked up six flights, bent over, and with difficulty unstuck the icon bundle from the bottom of the sofa.

"Here it is," I said. "It's in here. It had some chocolate stains at one point, but I think I got them off. Sorry. We didn't mean to take it. Peter thought it was a gift."

"We knew you had it."

"What will you do now?"

"Plant it in the dean's office and pretend it was just overlooked somehow. We'll probably try to blame it on one of the secretaries. He's constantly replacing them, anyway. It doesn't matter if they get reassigned."

"And what will happen to us?"

"You'll go home and start this cooperative agreement that you inexplicably managed to pull off."

"I'm not going to be arrested?"

"Arrested?"

"For taking the icon?"

"This?"

"It's extremely valuable from what I've understood."

He chuckled in a deadpan way.

"The dean's mistress gave it to him. She fancies herself an artist and painted it for him when they first started dating. She wouldn't be happy if it went missing, and she is extremely powerful. *Extremely* powerful. It's not the dean who decides when the secretaries will be replaced, if you catch my meaning."

"But I thought . . ."

"Listen. We're in the middle of a massive institutional restructuring process—course revisions, teaching resource reallocations, possible mergers. We don't know much about this process, but what we do know, for sure, is that some of us will be relocated to the university in Omsk. Are you familiar with Omsk?"

I shook my head.

"Siberia?"

I nodded.

"Omsk is in Siberia. It's the worst place in the world. Practically the gulag. That's why we contacted you guys in the first place. Ivan was familiar with your university because he attended a conference with someone from there, and we thought that if we could get a cooperation agreement in place, none of us would be relocated. We were the last three to be hired, and need some tangible results to show for ourselves. I mean, beyond our research. But then the icon went missing and since all three of us were in the room the last time it was seen, it pretty much guaranteed that one or all of us would be shipped off. We had to avoid that at all costs."

"Relocated? But aren't you a secret agent? Didn't you threaten to send me to the gulag? And you got our visas extended?"

He grinned.

"Irina's brother works in the visa office. All it took to get your visas extended was a bottle of vodka. And when it comes to threats . . ."

He came closer and looked down at me.

"You are a very irritating person. You laugh all the time, and you talk all the time, and you smile all the time. But it's all just an act. You're really sitting in a corner yelling jokes into the darkness. I don't know why. Maybe you're trying to distract the darkness. Maybe you're trying to distract yourself."

He ran his hand over my hair.

"Wisdom is better than folly, the way the light is better than the darkness."

I cried. Like I'd been crying for many months. The way I'd been crying since I was twelve and I didn't want to go home from school because I was afraid of what awaited me.

"You are a sparrow," he said. "You use up your energy from one moment to the next. On folly. On fear. On people who don't mean anything. What are you looking for?"

I cried even harder, but at the same time I began

to feel irritated. He didn't even know me, for Pete's sake. And if I was going to be compared to a bird, it certainly wasn't going to be a sparrow!

Until my irritation was replaced by a memory. I didn't know where it came from. I hadn't even known it was in there. But suddenly it rose up out of the darkness and into the light.

I was standing alone in the little store where I used to work on the weekends. Suddenly a sparrow flew in the open door. I didn't really have time to react, but I remember that I was scared it wouldn't get out. That it would fly into the window and hit its head. That it would attack and peck out my eyeballs. But it just swooped silently and elegantly above me through the room before it went back out, through the open door it had come in.

No one else saw it, and afterward I wondered if it might have been a dream. And I had forgotten it. Until now.

Pretty Putin looked into my eyes, abruptly put his arms around my waist, and pulled me to him. Soft lips met my own, and for a second there was nothing else. Just this kiss, which ensnared me, while the snowflakes danced around us. As if we were in a snow globe.

And then it was all over.

33

After a mechanical kiss at the airport, Bjørnar and I spent the next week packing, moving, and cleaning out the old house. We took possession of the new house, but it didn't really feel genuine. And once we were done transforming the old one into an empty, alien building, we stood motionless in what used to be our living room. There were a few things left on the floor that we didn't have any boxes left for or that we didn't want anymore—a lamp, a cutting board, a few pictures, some clothes hangers.

We had hardly said a word throughout the whole process, and we didn't say anything now, either. Just looked around. At a loss, as if wondering where we really belonged.

The awareness that I was responsible for forcing us out of this house and into a new one where we had no bearings also sat between us. And even though it felt like I had worked through something in Russia, it all reverted when I returned home. The house still hadn't sold. The iron fist still squeezed inside my chest. And I was probably still in danger of being transferred to the preschool-teacher education program, our own local version of Omsk.

Plus Bjørnar seemed to increasingly regard

me more like an annoying lab partner than a life partner. It was like he was Bobby Simone and I was Andy Sipowicz in *NYPD Blue*. Before they became good friends. Or after Sipowicz became an unpleasant alcoholic again. And before Simone found out that Sipowicz had been making out with Russians.

My first day back on the job there was a departmental meeting. I ran into Ingvill on my way down to the lecture hall. She was wearing a fluttering flannel cardigan, and had gone back to wearing her hair in pigtails. It was impossible to know if she planned to say anything to me, and I didn't know if I should say anything, either.

"Hi," I finally said.

"Whore," she said.

"Excuse me?"

"Whore. You're a W-H-O-R-E."

"What's wrong with you? Did you come down with Tourette's? I know you're trying to get me transferred to the preschool-teacher education program and I hate to tell you this, but *mindfuck* doesn't mean what you think it does. It means messing around with people's heads. It doesn't have anything to do with sex, OK?"

I took a step closer and stared hard into her dull eyes with a look I hope resembled the secret-agent look Pretty Putin had given me.

And I won. She backed down and scurried off

down the hallway. I slowly followed and found myself a seat way in the back so that I could sneak out just as soon as we had received our due recognition for having secured this gilt-edged cooperation agreement for the university.

People flocked in, but no one sat by me. Ingvill took a seat next to Frank very close to the front. Even closer to the front, the office manager was struggling to get the projector to work while the chair stood in the corner chatting quietly with Peter. It seemed like they were disagreeing about something, which made me a little nervous.

I hadn't told Peter the expensive icon wasn't priceless in the way we'd thought it was, mostly because it was completely irrelevant to our agreement. If I helped Peter with his icon problem, he was going to help with my preschool-teacher education program problem. That was our deal, and as far as I could see, I'd upheld my end of the bargain.

But now I noticed him casting furtive looks my way, and I didn't like that. Plus he kept touching the chair's arm, which wasn't reassuring, either. Why was he doing that?

Ultimately the chair sent Peter back to his seat, right next to Ingvill. As he sat down, he cast a glance back in my direction, one that seemed to be a blend of "Sorry" and "Good luck, kid." I pulled out my phone and sent him a text.

What did that look mean?
   Nothing.
What were you talking to the chair about?
   Nothing.
You remember our deal?

No response.
You remember our deal?

No response.
   Dickhead!!!
   :-)

"Hello, everyone. Welcome!" the chair said. "And a particularly warm welcome to our Russia delegation. The university has been trying to set up a collaboration with Saint Petersburg State University for years, and this year Peter finally accomplished this feat. Let's give him a big hand! I'll be sure to bring this up with the administration, Peter!"

The chair gave Peter the thumbs-up. He stood up halfway to accept the scattered applause.

"Thank you all," he said. "But I couldn't have done this without my colleague, Ingvill Christensen. She deserves a big round of applause as well."

He gestured with his hands to get a new round of applause going for Ingvill, who stood up and raised her arms in triumph, as I sat in the last row with my mouth open.

When the applause died out a few seconds later, Frank raised his hand.

"What about the rest of the English section?" he squeaked. "There were quite a few of us who wanted to be part of that delegation, you know. In the current climate, in these times of course revisions, internationalization is particularly precarious, and—"

"Yes, the English section," the chair said with a grin. "We have some good news there as well. Ingvill has been selected to join the preschool-teacher education program, and they are *really* looking forward to having her on board as the newest addition to their team. Another round of applause for Ingvill. Stand up, Ingvill!"

Ingvill reluctantly rose again, but this time she looked extremely confused, and mostly seemed to be trying to catch Peter's eye. He, however, stared fixedly at the floor.

This round of applause was much louder and lasted quite a bit longer than the one for the cooperative agreement, and Ingvill kept standing with her arms hanging limply at her sides until it died down. Then she opened her mouth.

"I just want to say," she said, in a shaky voice, "that this process wasn't fair. Or transparent. And that there are other people here in this department who should have been reassigned instead of me.

I'm not going to name names; I won't stoop to that. But you can be darn sure I'll be contacting the Office of the Auditor General. And then we'll see how this all turns out. I'm not some little cog in a machine! I'm not—"

"Yes, yes, Ingvill," the chair said, gesturing with her hand for Ingvill to take a seat. "We're sure you'll be very happy in your new position, and I think I speak for everyone when I say that we'll miss your cheerful presence. Oh, and Ingrid, I'm going to need the summary report for the Russia delegation from you. Ten pages by Friday. Thanks!"

I opened my mouth again but couldn't think of anything to say, so I closed it.

Shortly thereafter we were engulfed in yet another debate for and against the course revision, even though the preannounced subject of this meeting was a presentation of the results of the work environment study.

That was when I stood up with an apologetic smile and scanned the room for any kind of nod of approval, but as usual had to leave before one materialized. I took up position outside Peter's office and waited until he came squeaking down the hall five minutes later.

"I'm done playing on the team."

"What do you mean?"

"Am I wrong in thinking that you tried to convince the chair to banish me to the preschool-teacher education program instead of Ingvill? Completely counter to our agreement?"

He smiled wryly and shrugged.

"Ingvill won't last five minutes there," he said. "Do you know how much teaching they have to do? We managed to protect her here by making up about seventy percent of her work duties. Nonexistent reports and pseudoresearch. Mark my words, in the preschool-teacher education program she'll be out on a medical leave of absence for some made-up condition within six months. Laid off within a year. Besides, you'd have done just fine there."

"That's what *you* think."

He smiled again.

"Well, at least that's the end of the bad-cop strategy," I said. "From now on we're going to be pragmatic about the course revision and try to make the best of it."

He laughed.

"We gave up on that strategy ages ago! Now we have a new one. Frank tipped me off to it: Zen Connection. It's called Mindful Presence. It's about playfulness, motion, spontaneity, moments of connection."

"But Frank hasn't mastered any of those things."

"Now you're being a little unfair."

"Besides, the priority rankings are already done. Ingvill's being demoted to the preschool-teacher education program. There's nothing left to fight for!"

"Ah, that's where you're wrong! Just because the chair has decided to protect you, the battle isn't over. We're going to try to get Oddvar sent down there. *That's* the plan."

"I won't be part of anything like that. You can just forget about it."

"Honestly, Ingrid, that's not very collegial. I think *you* could benefit from some Mindful Presence training. Maybe that would give you a clearer idea of who is actually on your team. In addition to your own self, that is."

"I pulled off the cooperation agreement with Russia! The only one of its kind! Is no one going to thank me for that?"

He chuckled good-naturedly.

"That cooperation agreement only benefits the chair. Now there'll be four more years of her. But it means zilch to us. How many of our students are going to go to Russia? None! We don't offer any programs that have anything to do with Russia. I mean, would you go to Saint Petersburg to study Ibsen? Really, Ingrid, you're so naive."

"I'm not naive. I'm the bad cop!"

34

I eventually managed to convince both Alva's preschool teacher and Bjørnar that I wasn't an alcoholic. Yet I was informed that it would be preferable if my husband were responsible for preschool drop-off and pickup and that under no circumstances should I speak to Titus's au pair.

We eventually sold the house, too, to a young couple expecting their first child and living in a mildew-infested basement apartment way outside of town.

I watched them as they stood there looking around the kitchen.

"Look, a door opening right onto the backyard," she said, rubbing her belly. "Wouldn't that be nice?"

So, we sold. For five hundred thousand kroner below our asking price.

"You should have waited until May," the realtor said. "The 17th of May. The market's always really hopping by then."

" 'Really hopping' can't compete with stress cancer," I said.

"Sunk cost," Bjørnar said after sitting beneath the chandelier in the big new dining room for three days crunching numbers.

"What?"

"Money that's gone and can't be recovered so we don't need to think about it."

Sunk cost, I thought as I noticed the bottle of champagne that was still sitting unopened in the fridge. We were going to open it once we were settled. Once there was no longer any need to fear the monster lurking in the darkness below. Once Tehom had settled back down again.

But this was not that time.

Deep inside I knew that the panic attacks and the fear of death wouldn't let up until I had talked to Bjørnar about one last thing. It was just so hard to find a time and place that seemed right for a conversation that could potentially usher in the final doom. Which would be the impetus for my transformation into the cough-syrup lady.

So I kept my eyes and ears open and bided my time, waiting for the right moment.

Which turned out to be five minutes before Bjørnar was supposed to take Ebba to soccer practice.

I stood outside the bathroom, pounding on the door.

"Can I come in?" I yelled.

"I'm on the toilet in here. Can't you use the other bathroom?"

"No."

Five minutes later he opened the door.

"You know I don't like it when someone stands outside the door, waiting like that."

"I wasn't doing that!"

"Yes, you were. I could hear you breathing."

"Fine. I was. But I have to talk to you about something."

There was a pounding in my chest.

"I'm late. We're training for the merit badge. Everyone has to be able to do it."

"Yeah, but just hold on for a second. I did something."

He sighed.

"Don't sigh! That distracts me."

"OK."

"I did something dumb."

"And . . . ?"

"And the dumb thing was . . . You know how I went to Saint Petersburg?"

"Yes?"

"Right when we weren't doing so well?"

"Yes?"

"Well, not that we weren't doing so well, the two of us. Although actually we weren't doing that well, but obviously I knew that was because of all the stuff with the house, that we hadn't sold it yet and we were just so busy and . . . It was a stressful time and everything was so dark and gloomy and depressing. And then I got sick while I was there and I was taking some pretty strong medicine. You know, that cough syrup I told you about."

"Are you going to get to the point anytime soon?"

"Well, it's just that I'm really not looking forward to this . . ."

I waved my hands around in the air.

He looked at me.

"OK, I'm starting to get a little concerned. What did you do?"

I inhaled. Exhaled. Closed my eyes and clenched my flailing hands.

"I kissed a Russian! Or—I kissed him one time. And then he kissed me. One time. I'm sorry! It wasn't anything more than that, I promise! One kiss. Well, or two. Kind of depends on how you count. It didn't mean anything, but I'm very, very sorry and I'll never do anything like that again!"

Everything was still for a moment, completely still.

For a moment, my heart quit beating.

And I knew this was it.

This was the awful thing.

I tried to think positive thoughts, but it didn't work.

Now the seams ripped apart.

Now it was over.

Bjørnar started to laugh.

I opened my eyes.

"Why are you laughing?"

"I'm sorry. You're just so unexpected. I thought you were going to tell me something terrible."

"So you don't want to get divorced?"

283

"Divorced? No, you know there's no way we could afford that."

"But you *want* a divorce? You feel betrayed?"

"No."

My heart was beating; I could breathe. There was an effervescent sensation in my chest.

I stepped closer and wrapped my arms around him.

"Anyway, I'm sorry," I said. "I'll never do it again. Like I said."

"Fine. It's not cool to go around kissing other people. Certainly not Russians, anyway. What were you thinking? Was it Stockholm syndrome?"

"I didn't think of that. A mix of Stockholm syndrome and being hopped up on cough syrup, maybe."

"Well, I suppose we all have our skeletons in the closet."

"Our what? Wait, have *you* kissed someone else?"

"One time."

"When?"

He blushed a little.

"At the Christmas party."

"What Christmas party?"

"The office party at the Høyfjell Hotel. My first year out of law school. I had a little too much to drink. And I kissed Merethe from work."

"One time?"

"One time."

"Just that?"

"Just that."

I thought this over. Mulled over what had happened. Not a bomb blast, really. Not Nagasaki.

Actually balance, equilibrium.

Yin and yang. Harry and Sally. Hall and Oates.

A gift instead of a disaster.

So completely unexpected.

I kissed him. It was a kiss that had been repeated many times. It wasn't the same, but it wasn't different. It had the same warmth, taste, feeling, and consistency as the year before and ten years before that.

It was a kiss I felt at home in. Which *was* home.

Maybe I didn't need to be scared it would disappear. Maybe I could just be grateful. For right now.

"Are you guys going to suck face all day or what?" Ebba was in full soccer regalia, holding out her cell phone. "Come on, we're late. Jenny's standing by the front door waiting. You said we were going to give her a ride. Could you get a move on?"

"I'm coming," Bjørnar said. "Just had to do a little kissing with your mother first."

"How much do you love me?" I asked him.

"Six percent."

"Six percent?"

"Well, twenty-seven then."

"Twenty-seven percent? You love me ninety-seven percent, right? At least?"

He and Ebba walked out the door.

"To be or not to be," I called after him.

And as the door closed, he responded, "That is the question."